TRIPLE PEAKS

Patch-Eye Turrell was an outlaw who rode into Triple Peaks expecting to find a peaceful cattle range where his reputation as a killer was not known, and where he could transform the valley into a place of terror and fear. Within two months, the slickest bunch of outlaws that ever operated in the West was stealing the gold from the banks in the county — and no one dared to oppose them. But lawyer Wayne Thorpe sent for the right man to sort things out. Could Garth Martinue succeed?

GLEN NORTEN

TRIPLE PEAKS

Complete and Unabridged

LINFORD
Leicester

First hardcover edition published in Great Britain
in 2002, by Robert Hale Limited, London
Originally published in paperback as

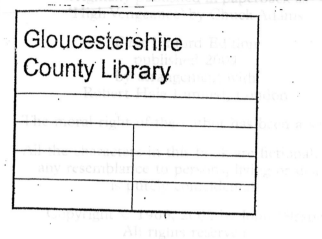

British Library CIP Data

Norten, Glen, *1928* –
   Triple peaks.—Large print ed.—
   Linford western library
   1. Western stories 2. Large type books
   I. Title II. Adams, Chuck. High vengenance
   823.9′14 [F]

   ISBN 1–84395–263–7

Published by
F. A. Thorpe (Publishing)
Anstey, Leicestershire

Set by Words & Graphics Ltd.
Anstey, Leicestershire
Printed and bound in Great Britain by
T. J. International Ltd., Padstow, Cornwall

This book is printed on acid-free paper

1

Outlaw

There was a steady, hurting, hammering thud inside Turrell's skull which throbbed worse every time his heart beat. It was something that hurt worse than anything he could recall, sickening, making it difficult for him to keep his grip on the reins. For the past ten minutes, his horse had plunged madly through thick pine and tangled underbrush; with snake-like branches, covered in thorns, lancing at him from the clinging darkness. But the pain with every heartbeat drowned out all other pain in his body and he scarcely felt the tearing of his flesh. He clutched desperately at the reins, hung on with his knees pressed tight into his horse's flanks.

Pain gripped him with fiery hands and made him want to vomit. His

1

muscles felt soft and useless like rubber. Behind him, he knew, the pursuit was getting under way. Horses had been commandeered, deputies recruited for the posse, and now they were less than half a mile behind him, gaining every second.

The night's cold air brought its own numbness to his arms and legs, but his shirt was soaked with sweat in spite of the cold. A single rifle-shot came sharp and clear as a whiplash as he broke out of the undergrowth into a wide clearing and he heard the slug whine past his head and smack into the thick bark of one of the nearby trees. The horse galloped on its way and he bent low in the saddle. On the far side of the clearing, he found a thin trail of sorts, but speed was out of the question now and off in the distance, on either side of him he could hear the crash of other riders flanking him.

Swiftly, acting on instinct, he reined up his mount, swung down from the saddle, his braced legs hitting the ground with a shock that sent agony searing through the muscles of his legs. Gritting his teeth, struggling to prevent the yell of pain from bursting forth from his lips, he dived for the nearest clump of bushes, veered off to his left for a couple of paces until he was crouched down among the thorny branches and pulled the sixgun from its holster. His horse came to a standstill among the brush some yards away, standing hipshot now that it was able to rest. He checked the impulse to run. To move out into the open now would be to invite disaster. He lay quite still, fighting for breath, eyes and ears searching the darkness for the slightest movement and the faintest sound.

'Damn it, he's got to be somewhere around,' bellowed a harsh voice which he recognized as belonging to Cantry, the sheriff from Culver City, the man leading the posse.

Turrell held his breath. Out of the corner of his eye, he had a glimpse of a compact knot of men. They had been skylined for only a brief fraction of a second, but that had been enough for him to spot them. They were moving slowly through the dense brush to his left, urging their mounts forward through the rough ground. Somebody's horse stumbled in one of the holes and fell, throwing its rider, causing shouts and yells and curses.

Turrell's lips pulled back in a vicious snarl. As he lay there, the gun gripped tightly in his right fist, his finger on the trigger, he remembered the events of that morning. Shortly after he had ridden into Culver City, he had spotted the wanted notice pinned outside the local jail. It had been an old poster, the picture on it bearing only a superficial resemblance to himself and he had decided that in spite of this, he would be safe enough in town for a few days. It had proved to be a wrong move. That goddamned bounty hunter had not been fooled by the age of the picture on the poster, had watched him for an hour or more while he had registered at the single hotel in the town, while he had eaten a leisurely breakfast, not making his move until he had stepped out on the street a couple of hours before noon. Then he had made his play, had almost taken him by surprise. Usually these bounty hunters shot their man in the back, took no chances themselves before claiming the reward money. But there had been a streak of bravado about this one and he had yelled a challenge just before he had pulled his gun. That yell had been the last sound he had made in this life. His Colt was still not clear of leather when the slug from Turrell's gun tore through his chest, sending him sprawling in the dust.

He had gone forward to check that the other was dead and, in that instant, he had been off guard. He had heard the soft movement of a man at his back, footsteps muffled by the dust, had half turned before the butt of a revolver had crashed down on to the back of his unprotected head. When he had come round, he was lying on a bunk in one of the cells of the town jail and Cantry, the sheriff, was staring at him through the bars. At first, his brain had been numbed by that smashing blow on the skull, then he had been able to think clearly. One look at Cantry's face and the poster in his hands had convinced him of the futility of trying to bluff his way out of the jail.

When Cantry had left for his evening meal, leaving the young deputy in charge of the jail, he must have figured that there would be no trouble because the deputy had fallen for the oldest trick in the book. Lying on the bunk, he had moaned sufficiently convincingly for the other to come running, open the door of the cell and bend down beside the bunk to examine him. Turrell's lips twisted back into another vicious grin as he recalled how the deputy had fallen hard against the wall of the cell when he had sent his fist crashing into the other's chin. Less than three minutes later, with the deputy trussed up on the bunk like a prize turkey, he had slipped out of the cell into the street, worked his way through some of the narrow, twisting alleys until he had come upon the livery stables. The groom had never known what had hit him as Turrell had come up behind him, cat-footed, slamming the butt of the deputy's gun on to the back of his head. He had taken the fastest looking horse in the stables, ridden out of town and headed west. How the posse had found his trail he did not know, unless they had an Indian guide with them, one of the braves who could smell a white man half a mile away and follow a horse's trail over rock, and in pitch blackness. But they had followed it and now they were busy beating the brush for him, with Cantry yelling orders at the top of his voice every few seconds.

* * *

A blast of gunfire came from the shadows over to his right. There was a shout, then silence. Whoever had fired that shot had been shooting at shadows, Turrell thought with a savage grimace. He squirmed back a couple of feet into the undergrowth, heard them moving again in his direction. He could see the head and shoulders of a man outlined against the skyline above the bushes on the far side of the clearing. More gunfire broke out, then Cantry yelled: 'Hold your fire, men! We'll never pick him out if we keep shooting like this. I want you to move around through the trees, then stop every fifteen seconds and listen. He's sure to give himself away soon.'

A voice that Turrell did not recognize sounded from the opposite side of the clearing. 'How'd you know he ain't ridden on through this goddamned brush, Cantry? He could be a couple of miles away, out in the open and headin' away from us every second.'

'We'd have heard his horse if he'd done that, Yacey. He's pulled off someplace in this brush.'

'I still figure he's outsmarted us. He could've walked his horse on out while we've been crashin' around here lookin' for him.'

'Yacey's right, Sheriff,' called another voice from the darkness. 'If he was hidin' around here he could've shot down some of us from cover.'

'Keep lookin',' called the other impatiently. 'If we don't smoke him out in five minutes we'll move on away.' Turrell eased himself further among the tall, rearing trees, making no sound. There was blood on the side of his head where a bullet had creased it, aggravating the wound caused by Cantry's gun butt. His left eye stung like fire and it was difficult to see through it properly. His vision seemed oddly blurred and at times double. He rubbed at it angrily with his knuckles, cursing softly under his breath. If it hadn't been for this posse coming up on him so fast, he could have been clear out of the county by now. He felt a slow trickle of ice-cold water soak into his shirt as he lay on his side, lifting himself up a little so that he would be able to get in a good shot at any of the men who came close to finding him. He could no longer see Cantry but he heard the snapping of dry twigs and the harsh wheeze of the sheriff's breath as he thrust his none too lissom form through the bushes. Turrell clearly heard the lawman's footfalls as he worked his way around the edge of the clearing. Sooner or later, he told himself, the other was going to spot his horse standing there in the shadows not more than fifteen feet away from where he lay and then they would know he was hidden somewhere around and nothing on earth would stop them from finding him eventually.

'There's a trail over here,' yelled a voice excitedly. 'Prints, too, but it's hard to say how fresh.'

There was a renewed movement in the brush. Cautiously, Turrell lifted his head to stare out into the blackness. At first he could make out nothing. Then, gradually, he was able to make out shapes and contours as they emerged from the overall darkness of the background. He sucked in a sharp breath, then lowered his head very slowly and carefully. There was a man standing less than three feet from him, his back to him, so close that Turrell had only to reach out with his hand to touch him. Gently, he lifted the gun in his hand, lined up the barrel on the man's back, his finger ready to squeeze the trigger if the other should turn to look behind him. How the man had got there without being seen or heard, he did not know.

'Over this way, Bill,' called Cantry harshly. 'He could've lit out along this trail; it leads over the ridge. Once he was down there we'd never hear him. Let's get after him.'

'What if he's along there waitin' in ambush?' asked one of the men in a low growl.

'Maybe he is,' snorted Cantry. 'But I figured I'd brought men with guts along with me in this posse. If there are any

11

more of you who feel scared, better pull out now and make your way back to town. I'm goin' to bring in Turrell dead or alive.'

'You sure it was Turrell?'

'Ain't no mistake about it. He's been wanted in half a dozen states for more'n two years now. That bounty hunter recognized him. That's why he was killed. Could be he figured he had the drop on this outlaw.'

There was a hoarse laugh from one of the men. Then Turrell heard them moving away into the brush and a moment later the man in front of his hiding place went off, not once turning his head to glance behind him.

When he was certain they had all gone, Turrell rose stiffly to his feet, thrust the Colt back into its holster and gingerly put up a hand to touch the side of his skull. He winced instinctively as his fingers touched the bruised, torn flesh. A lance of pain throbbed through his brain and he put out a hand to steady himself. He was hurt badly, he knew; and the sooner he got to a doctor who did not ask awkward questions, the better.

This country was new to him and he did not know how far he would have to ride before he reached another town like Culver City, where there might be the chance of getting his wounds treated. His hand reached down and he pressed the heavy money belt around his middle, a belt the law officers in Culver City had not found when they had knocked him out and dragged him off to their jail. There were sufficient golden dollars in it to tempt any doctor to help him and keep his mouth closed.

Following that trail which led west along the ridge was out of the question now. His best chance was to cut slowly through the brush at its thickest point until he came out into the open and then cut around to the west again, hoping to stay out of sight of that posse. How far those men would ride until they gave up the chase, he did not know. But from some of the remarks that had been passed when they had been searching the undergrowth for him, several of them had no heart for continuing the search for him.

Moving over to his horse, still standing silent and patient near the edge of the clearing, he somehow managed to swing himself up into the saddle. The pain in his skull had grown worse and it was all he could do to keep a tight grip on the reins and remain upright in the saddle as he gigged his mount forward into the dense brush. There was a solitary echo from far off to the west, but the sound was not repeated and he guessed that the posse was still working its way along the ridge, moving cautiously in case he was waiting in ambush, ready to shoot down the first one to get within range.

He rode forward nervously now that the first tension was over, easing slowly from his mind. When he finally came out into the open, he was scarcely prepared for it. One moment the trees lay thick in front of him, the next they had thinned and fallen behind him and there was a cold wind blowing directly into his face and the ground dropped away steeply in front of him. He pushed the horse headlong down the slope, sliding, crashing occasionally to its haunches, thrusting against the slender saplings which were the only growths now barring its path. He felt himself being half swept from the saddle several times and only succeeded in hanging on by the skin of his teeth, clutching desperately at the saddle horn.

As he rode, one part of his mind, detached from the rest, reasoned with an astounding clarity that this headlong plunge down the hillside must have taken him a valuable quarter of a mile from the wood and that if he could only continue until he was across the wide valley that stretched away in front of him, a palely shimmering flatness in the starshine, he would have sufficiently outdistanced his pursuers to be reasonably safe. The horse was tired. He could feel that by the way it staggered at times in its headlong run and there was little doubt that its feet would be sore from the thorny, uneven ground inside the trees. But he had chosen it carefully from among those in the livery stables, knew that it was undoubtedly of thoroughbred stock and would be able to outrun most of the horses on his trail, especially if it were being pushed. And it was being pushed now. He did not like the way he had occasionally to dig in the rowels of his spurs, but it was essential that he should put as much distance between his pursuers and himself before dawn. The horse drew back its lips over the bit, surged forward gallantly, battling down the steep hillside, among the scattered boulders at the bottom.

They hit the edge of the flats in a series of bounding, leaping strides, and now Turrell leaned low in the saddle, crouching down over the horse's neck, easing his weight as much as possible in the stirrups, struggling to prevent himself from losing consciousness. He knew instinctively that he had lost a lot of blood, that the wound on the side of his skull was still bleeding and it was only a matter of time before he passed out and slipped from the saddle. A few times, his hold slipped and he almost slithered sideways and in those frightening moments, his blood threatened to freeze in his veins and he would jerk upright in the saddle, waiting fearfully for the tragedy. But it never came. Somehow, he managed to hang on to his buckling consciousness and it seemed that the bay had run across the mesa in no time at all.

An hour later, with the moon lifting clear of the eastern horizon, a great slice of yellow that threw a pale, cold light over the terrain, he was riding through some of the roughest country he had ever known. The going was more difficult hereabouts, the horse more tired than before, and there were several times when it wanted to halt and only moved on because he raked his spurs along its flesh.

Fifteen minutes later, he swung the horse off the trail, through a thickly tangled area of catsclaw and mesquite, into a clump of vine-festooned trees where he reined to a halt and let it blow. The mount became hipshot at once, but its head was still high and the only sound was the great wheezing of air in and out of the animal's lungs. Leaning back in the saddle, he reached for his tobacco pouch, twisted himself a cigarette, lit it and drew the smoke gratefully into his lungs. Even as he smoked, he turned his head slowly from side to side, his mind and senses alert to any unexpected sound in the dark moonthrown shadows among the rocks and trees nearby. In the yellow moon-light, vague shapes seemed to move among the rocks and more than once, he felt the cold sweat break out on his body at a sudden sound as some noctural creature moved through the mesquite.

When he was sure that there was no pursuit, he slid from his saddle, finished his smoke, then took a long drink from his water bottle. Unfastening the cinch from beneath the horse's belly, he pulled off the saddle, tethered the mount so that it had room in which to graze, set out his blanket and stretched himself out on the hard earth, resting his head on the saddle. The weariness in his body was so great that he was asleep almost at once.

★   ★   ★

When he woke it was still dark, but the moon had drifted across the heavens and was now glinting yellowly at him from behind the waving branches of the trees at his back. He lay for a moment staring up at the starlit heavens, then sat up suddenly as the horse uttered a soft, warning whinney. Out of the corner of his eye, he noticed that there was a pale strip of grey along the eastern horizon where the dawn was just beginning to brighten, the stars fading in that direction. The horse gave a faint murmur of sound once more and with an effort, he staggered to his feet, moved forward very quietly.

He thought he heard an answering sound from somewhere in the darkness below him, but he could not be sure. The wind seemed to be carrying several vagrant sounds up to him through the blackness. For a long moment, he remained crouched at the lip of the ledge peering down into the darkness. Then a harsh shout, echoing clearly, reached him and switching his gaze, he saw the rider come out into the open some four hundred yards away and sit quite still in the saddle, staring up at the ledge. Turrell resisted the urge to pull his head down sharply. The other could not see him against the background of trees and rock even though he was probably staring straight at him. Presently, more men rode out and joined the other. They were too far away for Turrell to recognize any of them definitely, but he did not need to see their faces to know who they were.

Cantry and the posse. Somehow, he had swung around the valley and come on him from the south. They appeared to be conferring among themselves and one of them broke off to point in Turrell's direction. He guessed they were discussing the direction in which they should continue their search for him. He doubted if they could have picked up his trail, even in the moonlight. Pure luck would have brought them so close to him.

Edging back into the trees, he threw the saddle back on to the horse, pulled the cinch tight under its belly, then hauled himself weakly into the saddle, pulling hard on the reins as he walked the horse back among the trees, away from the ridge. Once out of the grove, he deliberately rode over the roughest, hardest ground he could find determined to leave no prints for the posse to follow. Riding down into another long, narrow valley, he chose a wrinkle-edged ravine and rode through it, his mount's shoes striking hard on the solid rock underfoot. The steep-sided walls rose sheer on either side of him, shutting him in, but providing him with cover at the same time. Threading his way over the gravelly bed of the ravine, through the high-walled rock fissures, moulded in a bygone age, he came out of the ravine, just as the grey glow in the east was beginning to be tinged with red as the sun lifted just beyond the horizon.

In his mind, he was not exactly sure what he was going to do even if he did manage to keep ahead of Cantry and his men. How far the lawman's jurisdiction stretched beyond Culver City, he didn't know. But he figured that the other had only to mention to the sheriff of the next town who the stranger was and he would either find himself in jail again or have to fight his way out. At the moment, in his weakened state, he did not relish either course.

His shadow ran behind him, shorter and shorter as the sun lifted clear of the horizon, red at first but soon brightening to yellow and then white. He drowsed now in the saddle, head falling forward on to his chest, the throbbing in his skull having subsided into a dull, continuous ache now that was almost as agonising as the pain he had felt earlier. Gradually, the country lifted from its flatness and he rode into a more rugged stretch of ground, interspersed with huge boulders and rising sandstone buttes that glowed redly in the fierce sunlight. Slowly, the heat head reached its piled-up intensity. The bright flaming splashes as the sunlight struck the metal parts of his bridle, sending them lancing into his eyes only served to increase the hurt in his mind and body. Stirring himself, he reversed his neckpiece over the lower half of his face. There was still a hot wind blowing across this desert place, sending stray eddies whirling over the ground, kicking up the itching, irritating grains of dust into his face, clogging eyes and ears and nose, getting into his mouth and nostrils.

Here and there among the rolling dunes and dry clay gulches, he came across a lone pine tree which stood as a warning sentinel to the hills which now lay sprawled across the skyline to the west. Bulky and high, they lifted their long, undulating length above the desertlands, looming over them. But as the long morning dragged by on leaden, heat-filled feet with the sun climbing to its zenith and then beginning on the long, slow slide down to the west, the hills seemed just as far away from him as they had been when he had started out towards them shortly after dawn.

But the flat country enabled him to keep an eye on the trail at his back and the further he rode, the more convinced he was, that he had thrown the posse off the scent by heading out in this direction. He saw no tell-tale grey clouds of dust behind him which would have indicated a group of hard-riding men. Gradually, he allowed the horse to slow its pace and it picked its way forward with head lowered.

Shortly before three o'clock in the afternoon, with the terrible, scorching heat bringing the sweat boiling out on his body, mingling with the dust on his flesh, he came in sight of a narrow creek, shallow but still with water flowing along the bottom of it, over a smooth stone bed. He climbed stiffly and wearily from the saddle, went down on to his stomach, forced himself to ignore the beating pain in his skull as he stretched out and half-buried his face under the water. He drank thirstily, washed some of the dust from his face, felt the mask crack and his face sting as the water touched the scorched flesh beneath. Finished, he filled his water bottle, then let the horse drink, watching as it pushed its muzzle completely under the water to drink, a sure sign of a thoroughbred.

Wetting his bandana, he tried to wipe away most of the dried blood which had congealed on the side of his head. His left eye still felt as if it were on fire and the brilliant sunlight sent stabs of pain lancing through into his skull whenever he tried to focus it on anything. That blow on the head, or the slug which had creased his forehead, must have done something to it, he decided after a while. Climbing, stiff-legged, to the top of a low rise, he stared back along the way he had come. The desert was empty and the middle-down sun burned on the back of his neck and shoulders like an open flame, turning the distant horizons a bluish-yellow that was hurting to the vision. The ground shimmered all about him as if he were viewing it through a layer of constantly moving water.

Satisfied that there was no one on the trail, he went back to the creek, stretched himself down in the shade of one of the rocks, pulled his hat down over his eyes, and forced himself to relax, grateful for the chance to rest a while and do a little thinking. So far he had been on the run to clear himself from the weight of the posse that Sheriff Cantry had got up against him, well knowing that he could never have bucked the whole outfit even if he had managed to take them from ambush and by surprise.

He experienced again his hatred of the world, his contempt for the law which had hounded him across half a dozen states. All he wanted now was to get someplace where he was not known, where he could build up a band of men who could defy the law. He had led such a band once, but the Texas Rangers had smashed them, trapped them in a gully which had overlooked the railroad. There had been more lawmen riding the train they had intended to rob and he had been the only one to escape with his life. Two other members of the gang, badly injured in the gunfight, had been taken to Tucson, tried, and hanged for their part in the attempted hold-up. Now there was a reward of five thousand dollars for the capture of Ed Turrell, dead or alive. He turned slightly on the ground, lay on his side, closed his eyes and was asleep within moments.

When the sunlight came around the edge of the rock, burning in his eyes, he woke, stretched himself, drank from the creek once more, then bent to tighten the cinch, climbed up into the saddle and put his mount to the narrow, rocky trail on the far side of the creek. In time, the trail widened and he reached a stage road, clearly marked by the imprint of the wheels in the dusty earth. Gigging his mount, he started the slow climb into the benchlands of the hills, now dark and shadowed by the setting sun. As he rode, the heat of the day was dissipated by the flowing coolness that swept down at him from the hills. He breathed it in with grateful breaths, filling his lungs with it, feeling the sweat turn cold on his back and chest. The horse increased its gait as if sensing that they were close to the end of the trail.

Just as the sun vanished behind the

looming crests of the hills, the sky and the world turning blue all about him, filled with the night smells of the tall hills and ridges, he turned a bend in the trail and came in sight of the town, perhaps half a mile distant, on the far side of a wide river that wound down from the point where it was born high in the hills.

The town was set out in a haphazard manner on a wide bench of flat ground which fronted the desert and was backed by the looming backdrop of the hills. The main street was a continuation of the trail which he had followed for the past two hours. It ran arrow-straight through the centre of the town, dividing it into two almost equal halves, and then disappeared into the gloom that lay across the foothills.

The long shadows lay deep on the town as he rode over the narrow wooden bridge that spanned the river. Here and there, he saw a yellow light in a window of one of the wooden shacks which lined the main street of the town.

There were few men on the street for it was almost supper time and he guessed that most of them were in the restaurants and saloons. As he walked his mount slowly along the street, he kept switching his gaze from side to side until he spotted the place he was looking for. The faded wooden sign above the door said: 'Clancy Foster, MD.'

Making a mental note of its position, he rode on until he came to the livery stables where he dismounted, led his horse inside. A weather-beaten individual drifted out of the gloom at the rear of the building, gave him a glance of open curiosity, then took the reins as Turrell held them out to him.

'The terms are a dollar fifty a day,' grunted the other surlily.

'I'll probably be ridin' on out tomorrow,' Turrell said. He handed over two dollars. 'Throw in an extra feed and a rub down.'

The groom glanced at the coins, then nodded slowly, led the horse away to the stalls. Turrell went out into the street, stood with his back against one of the wooden posts and rolled himself a smoke. The dust in his throat, lining it all the way down, gave the smoke no flavour, but it gave him the opportunity to watch the street and survey the town, eyes alert for trouble.

During the ten minutes that he stood there in the shadows, he saw only three men in the street. One lit out of town as if all the devils in hell were at his back. The other two moved slowly across the street from one of the small eating houses to the saloon. There was a cool current of air flowing along the main street now and it took the sting of the day's heat from him. Dropping the stub of the cigarette on to the ground, he crushed it out under his heel, moved off along the street to the doctor's place. Rapping sharply on the door, he waited. For a long moment there was no sound inside the building and he was on the point of knocking again when the light snapped on in the room and there was a sound of footsteps just beyond the door. It opened a moment later and he saw the pale grey blur of a face peering out at him, eyes wide behind a pair of steel-rimmed glasses.

'Who is it?' queried a harsh voice.

'Open up,' Turrell said hoarsely. 'I need your help.'

The other hesitated, then opened the door and stood to one side for him to enter. The doctor glanced hurriedly up and down the street before closing the door behind him.

'Go through into the room,' said the other, pointing the way.

Turrell stepped inside, blinking against the light of the lamp on the table. Then he turned and eyed the other intently. There was a look of veiled suspicion on the doctor's lean features, then his gaze drifted to the guns in Turrell's holsters and his lips tightened a shade.

'What is it you want of me?' asked the other. The dignity was a little too contrived.

'I need some doctorin',' grunted

Turrell. 'That sign outside means you're a doctor, doesn't it?'

'That's right.' The other moved forward as Turrell removed his hat. Then he nodded slowly. 'You'd better sit down and I'll take a look at that. What was it? A bullet?'

'Both that and a knock on the head from a gun butt,' Turrell said. He sat down in the chair at the table, blinked against the lamplight. The doctor noticed this but gave no outward sign. Going over to the door leading into the other room, he paused sharply as Turrell said thinly: 'Hold it there, Doc. Where do you reckon you're goin'?'

Foster shrugged his shoulders, kept his hand on the doorknob. 'I'll need my instruments for this. You seem strung up about something, stranger. A posse on your trail?'

'Why'd you say that?' For a moment, Turrell's right hand hovered close to the butt of the Colt at his waist. The other's expression did not change as he noticed the movement. There was a faint smile on his thin lips as he said calmly: 'You've got that hunted look about you, mister. There's the smell of gunsmoke on you.' He opened the door slowly. 'Don't worry. I don't intend to give you away to the sheriff. So far as I'm concerned, you're just here for treatment. That's as far as it goes with me.'

With an effort, Turrell forced himself to relax. 'Go ahead and get your instruments,' he said tautly. 'But no tricks, or you'll regret it.'

The other disappeared into the other room, came back a minute later with a black bag which he set down on the table in front of him. 'I'll boil some water and then take a look at that head wound.'

Turrell lifted his left hand and touched the side of his skull gingerly. It still hurt as he ran his fingertips over the torn flesh, but it had stopped bleeding. Sucking in a sharp breath, he watched closely as the other busied himself with a pan of water on the fire in the wide hearth. When it was boiling, he poured it into an enamel basin, carried it over to the table. Dipping the corner of a towel into the water, he began to bathe the side of Turrell's head. Pain tore through his skull and it was all he could do to keep himself from crying out aloud with the sheer agony of it. Gritting his teeth, he tasted salt on his lower lip where he had bitten into it. His hands were clenched so tightly that the nails dug deeply into the flesh of his palms, but he was scarcely aware of the pain.

'You're lucky to be still alive,' said the other after a pause. 'An inch to the right and that slug would have gone through your brain.'

'Could be that's what they were aimin' to do,' he muttered grimly.

'I sort of figured you'd been in a gunfight,' went on the other softly. He hesitated, then said: 'That eye of yours. Does the light hurt you when you look at it?'

'Seems like it's on fire.'

The doctor stepped back from the table, then held up the forefinger on his right hand. 'Close your right and watch my finger with your left,' he ordered. 'Keep watching it.'

Gently, he moved his finger from one side to the other. Turrell tried to follow the movement, then drew in a sharp intake of air as a stab of agony lanced through his head.

Nodding, Foster said: 'That slug must have caused more damage than you thought. Probably it glanced off the skull bone before tearing through the skin. Can you see properly out of it, or does everything look blurred and dim?'

The question was almost a physical shock to Turrell. He turned his head swiftly and stared at the other. 'You've got somethin' on your mind, Doc. What is it?'

'I'm afraid you're going to lose the sight of that eye, mister. I've seen cases like this before.'

Turrell said nothing for a long moment. He was vaguely aware of the numb, throbbing ache inside his head, like a hammer striking a continuous tattoo on a padded wall. Gradually, the news penetrated his mind. 'You mean I'm goin' to be blind?'

'Only in the one eye. The other is perfectly all right.' Foster smiled thinly. 'Try to tell yourself that you're lucky to be still alive. I think I can guarantee that you'll soon get over the other wound. A week or so and you won't know you've had it.'

Turrell felt the sweat on his face, trickling down his cheeks and running into his eyes. When Foster had finished dressing his wound, he got to his feet, swaying a little and holding on to the edge of the table to steady himself.

'You'd better stay here for the night,' suggested the other. 'In your present condition you won't get very far.'

'How much do I owe you for this, Doc?' he said harshly, as if he had not heard what the other had said.

Foster shrugged his shoulders. 'A couple of dollars,' he said tightly.

Turrell pulled the coins from his pocket and tossed them on to the table in front of him. Turning abruptly on his heel, he strode to the door, jerked it open with a savage movement, walked quickly along the hall and out through the street door into the dusk. He needed a drink.

His footsteps echoed hollowly on the wood-slatted boardwalk as he moved along the fronts of the buildings. Pushing open the swing doors of the saloon, he went inside. There were a couple of men standing at the bar and four more seated around one of the tables playing faro. He gave them a cursory glance, then walked to the bar, lifted a finger to the barkeep and waited for the drink to come. He took the whiskey quick, poured another and lingered over this one. The raw spirit burned his throat, but it made him feel better.

Back in the street, he caught the odour of food from the eating house on the corner of the street and the effect on him was so sharp that it was almost a physical pain in his mouth. A small group of men strolled out of the place as he made to go in, brushing closely by him. They all gave him bright-sharp glances that were quite noticeable things, making him wonder a little. Had any men from Culver City arrived here before him? There had seemed to be more than just interest in their looks.

He passed inside, chose a table where he could both watch the door and see through the window, and let the stiffness of a long day in the saddle seep slowly from his taut muscles and limbs. It felt good to sit and stretch his legs beneath the table. The place was almost empty now. Most of the tables were clean and near the counter there were only three still with the supper dishes piled on them. He noticed all this in the few moments before the Chinese cook came over.

'Got anythin' left to eat?' Turrell asked.

'Some,' agreed the other. His features

bore the Oriental's inscrutability. If he considered that Turrell was a stranger and wondered about the bandage on his head, he showed no sign whatever. 'Lamb stew, fried potatoes, cabbage.'

'Everythin',' Turrell said. 'I'm starvin'. It's been a long day on the trail.'

'Coming in five minutes.' The other backed away, disappeared around the edge of the counter. When he came back, he placed a heaped plate of stew and vegetables in front of him, brought salt and bread, paused for a moment, then said: 'Coffee or whiskey, mister?'

'Coffee. Black.'

He ate ravenously, realising for the first time how long it had been since he had eaten a decent meal, able to take his time over it. Finishing the stew, he dabbed the bread into the gravy, wiping the plate clean with it before sitting back in his chair and sipping the hot, strong coffee. One of the men seated at a table a few yards away, was staring at him curiously. He dropped his gaze as Turrell glanced in his direction.

Inwardly, he told himself that it was too dangerous a place to stay for long. Too close to Culver City and Cantry. Word could get here at any time that Ed Turrell, the outlaw, was somewhere in the territory, warning every lawman in the county to keep a look out for him.

Going across to the counter, he tossed a couple of coins down, then said to the Chinese cook: 'You know of any place in town where a man could get a bed for the night?'

'Sure thing.' The other nodded his head vigorously. 'There's a rooming house along the street, thirty yards maybe.'

'Thanks.' Turrell walked out through the swing doors, found the two-storied house and went inside. A meek-looking man sat behind the desk in the lobby. He gave Turrell a hard glance, clamped his teeth around the stub of the cigar between his lips.

'You got a room for the night?' he asked curtly.

A moment's hesitation while the

other looked him over, obviously trying to make up his mind about him. Then the man nodded abruptly. 'Sure. Five dollars for the night. That includes breakfast in the morning.'

'I'll take it.' Turrell placed the coins down on the desk, took the keys that the other offered him and went up the creaking stairs. At the top, there was a short corridor leading away into darkness with only a solitary lamp burning yellowly and dimly at the head of the stairs. The clerk had said that his room was at the very end. Making his way forward, he unlocked the door, went inside and turned the key in the lock after him. For a moment he fumbled in the dark, then went over to the window, glanced out. It faced the back of the building, he noticed, looked down on to a wide, rubbish-filled yard that brooded in the stillness.

Satisfied, he pulled the heavy curtains across the window, then went back into the room, struck a match and lit the lamp on the side table. There was water in the jug on the bureau and a basin. Stripping off his jacket and shirt, he poured half of the water into the basin and splashed it over his face and shoulders, let it run down his chest. It felt cool and good, shocked a little of the life back into his bone-weary body. The mask of dust on his face cracked as the water touched it and when he rubbed himself dry with the rough towel he found near the bed, his skin burned and itched. Unbuckling the heavy gunbelt, he laid it down on the chair at the bedside, took off his boots, then stretched himself out on top of the bed, hands clasped at the back of his neck. The doctor had done a good job on the wound along the side of his head and although it was still hurting to look out of his left eye, the pain was bearable now.

For a brief moment, he found himself wondering about Cantry and the posse which had trailed him most of the way from Culver City until he had succeeded in losing them that morning. But his mind and body were too weary to keep on thinking about them and a few moments later, he was asleep.

2

Heat Head

Ed Turrell came awake, sharply and abruptly an unguessable time later. Silently, moving with an animal-awareness that had saved his life on several past occasions, he shifted his position on the low bed, then swung his legs equally silently to the floor, got to his feet and reached out a stealthy hand towards the gunbelt hanging over the back of the chair. The lamp still burned on the small table and moving forward, he cupped his hand over the top and blew out the flame.

The sound which had somehow reached down into that part of his mind that never slept, came again and this time there was no mistaking it. The soft, stealthy noise of footsteps along the corridor outside his door. It could have been some other guest at the place, coming in after a long night in one of the saloons, trying to get to bed without waking up the entire place. But deep inside, Turrell knew that this wasn't the case. There was something about those soft movements outside that spelled danger. A brooding silence in the building only enhanced the furtive sounds. In the darkness, he saw the strip of yellow light that showed under his door. It grew brighter even as he watched it. Someone was carrying a lamp with them.

Soft-footing it over to the door, he pressed himself against it, listened intently. There were voices somewhere in the distance, at the far end of the corridor, he reckoned. Turrell stiffened. If somebody was looking for him; if that lawman Cantry had ridden on into this town and started asking awkward questions about any strangers who might have ridden in during the day. Maybe that doctor had talked. Maybe the bartender or that Chinese cook. He heard the door of the room next to his open and heavy footsteps moving around. The murmur of voices grew louder and he was able to make out some of the words. 'You're sure he took the other room?'

A mumbling voice said something Turrell did not catch, but he knew that it must have been the clerk who spoke. 'Guess he's asleep by now. Hardy and Vickers, take up positions along the corridor just in case he tries to make a run for it. The rest of you come with me. If we play this right, nobody is goin' to get hurt.'

Swiftly, snatching up his shirt and jacket, he pulled them on, then went over to the window, twitched back the curtains and peered down into the darkness, a blackness that was sharpened by the myriad points of diamond light that glittered in the heavens over the town. It was a long way to the ground and he knew that if he tried it by clambering down the narrow pipe against the wall he would almost certainly break a leg if not his neck. The handle of the door was turned. Then Cantry's voice sounded: 'We know you're in there, Turrell. Better open up before we blast the lock.' Knuckles rapped loudly on the door.

Casting about him, Turrell spotted the sheets on the bed. They would make an excellent rope if he tied them together. Knotting one end to the bedstead, he hauled the other sheets from the bed, twisted them and then tied each securely to the other, moved the bed carefully to the window, lowered the rope over the sill. The knocking on the door came again, then Cantry's voice yelled: 'Stand back from there, Clem.' Five seconds passed, then the sound of three gunshots ripped through the clinging silence. Turrell waited no longer. Swinging himself over the ledge, he lowered himself swiftly to the ground, dropping the last five feet to land on his hands and knees. The light appeared in the upstairs room and as he ran for the far side of the yard, he heard a harsh cry from above him:

'There he is. Over there!'

A gun roared and then another. The men who had moved over to the window began firing down at him. Down below, Turrell heard more shouting and bullets smacked against the wooden uprights, splintering chips from them. Something stung his face as he ran, then crouched down behind one of the posts, risking a couple of shots at the lighted window. He could see the silhouettes of the men, clearly visible against the yellow lamp-light. Guns were roaring continuously now, but in the midst of that sound, he heard one of the men let up a great cry and saw a shadow at the window suddenly tilt forward, slump over the window ledge and then fall into the yard. The spitting tongues of flame and the hellish racket was all about him now as he pushed himself to his feet and ran along the narrow alley that led away from the rear of the building. He reckoned that he was moving back into the outskirts of the town, away from the main street and that if he was to get to the livery stable and find his horse, he would soon have to turn and cut back.

Running around the angle of a low, slant-roofed building, he came out into a wider alley. There was a single door set in the side of the building. He tried it, rattling at the handle, but it was locked and he ran on, his breath rasping harsh and hot in his throat. Footsteps sounded in the near distance and there was a sudden bout of yelling as his pursuers ran into the alley he had just left.

Another low building loomed up in front of him. Again, the door was locked, but there was a wooden-shuttered window nearby. He clawed at it, breath whistling through his tightly clenched teeth. The shutters resisted him and in desperation, he thrust the barrel of the Colt between the two shutters and levered. For a moment nothing happened, then the rotten wood split with a sharp crack and he was able to thrust his hand inside, locate the catch and drag open the windows. With a savage heave of arm and shoulder muscles, he hauled himself inside, dropped to the floor and crouched down, holding his breath until it hurt in his lungs as the sound of footsteps came nearer. Pressing himself close to the cold wall, he listened to the uproar outside in the alley.

'Damn it, men,' roared Cantry. 'He's got to be around here someplace. He can't have reached the street or the rest of the boys would have spotted him and started shooting. Spread out and search every house.'

Letting his pent-up breath go in small pinches through his nostrils, Turrell moved carefully across the room, feeling ahead of him with outstretched hands. The smell of dust in this long abandoned place was irritating in his nostrils and he started suddenly, jerking the gun around as something small and invisible in the blackness scurried across the floor with a scratching of claws on the wood.

His fingertips touched solid wood. Slowly, he worked his way along the far wall until he found a door, jerking it open and stepping through. There was a window directly ahead of him, a faint square of light that stood out from the darkness on either side and he went quickly towards it, cursing under his breath as his shin struck the edge of a heavy table.

Peering through the window he found himself looking out on to the main street, knew that the narrow alley had brought him back further than he had reckoned. Releasing the catch on the window, he placed his fingers under it, levered it up gently. Time and rain had warped the wood and it was jammed in the frame. He would have to risk breaking the glass with his gunbutt. Lifting it carefully, he was on the point of breaking the window pane, then abruptly, he jerked himself back against the wall. The dark shadow fell across the window and he heard the hollow echo of the man's boots on the slatted boardwalk immediately outside. The man stopped and Turrell looked anxiously through the window. The man had stopped with his back to him, was looking out across the street. A moment later there was the scrape of a match, a brief orange flare. The cigarette lit, the man hesitated for a moment longer, then moved off. The sound of his footsteps died away into the distance. Turrell waited for a few seconds longer, then slammed the butt of the Colt against the glass. The crash sounded terribly loud in the stillness but was almost instantly drowned by the blast of scattered shots from somewhere at the back of the building.

A single shadow broke from the boardwalk as Turrell pushed his way through the smashed window into the street. Turrell pressed himself tightly against one of the uprights. The man had not seen him but he was clearly suspicious. It was just possible that he had heard the sound of the breaking glass and was trying to determine from where it had come. There was no one else in the street but this single man who came on slowly and stubbornly until he was only fifteen feet from where Turrell stood and there he stopped, head forward a little, his right hand hovering close to the gunbutt in his belt, trying to push his sight into the darkness in front of the building. He seemed to be staring straight at Turrell, not seeing him, but wary and cautious.

There was a delay, after which the man moved forward again. He had drawn his gun now, was edging along the front of the building. A moment later, his foot crunched on one of the scattered fragments of glass. Turrell saw him stiffen abruptly; then, carefully, the man moved to the window. For a moment, his back was towards him and in that instant, Turrell struck. The butt of the revolver caught the other on the skull just behind the left ear. He collapsed without a moan on to the boardwalk.

Turrell did not wait to examine him. Without pausing, he ran across the street towards the livery stable. A light came on inside the saloon as he ran. Somebody yelled an inquiry as a fresh blast of gunfire came from a different direction, the stabbing stiletto of orange light just visible in the shadows. Turrell felt the wind of the bullet as it fanned his cheek, ran on without breaking his stride. The swathe of light from the saloon, shining out across the street was a death trap. In it, he recognized at once, a man would be a perfect target to men hiding in the shadowed mouths of the alleys.

Not able to run directly to the stable, he was forced to run diagonally to one side. There was a strand of wire that ran from one side of a post fence to another and he squirmed under it, wriggled on his belly for a couple of yards, then vanished into the shadowed interior of the very stables. A horse whinnied loudly from one of the stalls, giving his position away.

From the far side of the street, close to the saloon, a man shouted: 'He must have headed into the stables. Fan out, men, and stop him!'

Working feverishly, he located the thoroughbred, threw the saddle that rested on the post over the animal, tightened the cinch, then swung up, hauling hard on the reins. There was only the one way of getting out of the stables and that would inevitably bring him into full view of the running men. But he would have to make a break for it now or they would pin him down and pick him off from three sides.

Kicking spurs along the horse's flanks, he crouched low over its neck as they plunged out into the street. He was seen instantly. A volley of ragged revolver shots crashed out from both sides of the street. Something seared along his arm but he gritted his teeth, kept low in the saddle, running the gauntlet of that fire. Out of the corner of his eye, he saw two men run from the shadows into the middle of the street directly in front of the horse. They had their guns lifted, hoping to shoot him out of the saddle. He jerked up the Colt in his right hand instinctively, loosed off a couple of shots, saw one of the men pitch forward on to his face in the dust. The other got off one shot before a slug tore into his leg. The man twisted under the leaden impact of the bullet as his leg bent. He went down on to one knee, lifted the gun to fire again, then jerked himself upright, his pale face bearing a look of stupified amazement as he remained stiff and taut for a few seconds, then slumped forward, his head dropping to one side as Turrell rode past him.

A few desultory shots followed him along the street, but he was in the clinging darkness now, a scarcely seen target and the men at his back were firing blind. There was a roaring in his ears like the thunder of a vast waterfall as he straightened up in the saddle and let his mount have its head. It did not need any urging, seeming to realise that they were in a hurry. Ears lying back, tail high, it galloped out of the town, over the rickety wooden bridge spanning the river, out into the benchlands that lay between the town and the rough desert.

He meant to skirt the hills, ride around them, knowing that in the darkness it would take the best part of a day for Cantry and his men to try to head through the hills and cut him off. He did not pause in his headlong flight across the desert until just before dawn, when he considered that he had outridden any pursuit. Sensing that the hard run was over, the horse slowed to a walk. Threading their way through the dried-up bed of a river which had cut a way through a narrow, steep-sided ravine, they came out into the open again as high over them, the crests of the hills to the west were just beginning to reflect the first light of dawn, even before the sky to the east showed any greyness.

Pausing for a while at the northern

end of the hills, he rested up for half an hour in a clump of tall trees on top of a knoll of ground which afforded him a commanding view of the surrounding territory. Unless the posse had taken to the hills they were some distance behind him, for in all of that time, he saw no sign of them. The dawn brightened swiftly to the east. Shadows lay among the rough boulders and long before the sun came up above the skyline, there was a rich yellow glow on the crests of the rising hills.

Climbing back into the saddle, he followed a narrow trail, deliberately riding the mount over hard, exposed areas of rock where no hoofprint would show and after a couple of miles of this riding the rimrock, he cut down into the broad stretching valley that lay spread out ahead of him, in the shadow of the ridge of hills. He was not exactly sure what he was going to do now, but he had the vague notion that he would have to keep on riding west if he was to reach a place where nobody knew him, where his name and reputation had not gone ahead of him. It could be that Cantry would follow him clear across the west, but somehow he did not think so. A sheriff had only a limited jurisdiction and once he went beyond his area of influence, he could do very little.

A wave of sunlight broke over the hills, scattering the darkness and the shadows of the night, and the suddenness of it was so rapid that for a moment, he was forced to blink his eyes against it and felt once more that stab of agony in his injured eye. Above the trail, the pines stood massed like a dark green curtain and at this hour, the air was so thin and clear that it was possible to make out the mountains in the far distance, more than fifty miles away, without any of the shimmering which would come as soon as the heat began to lift above the plains.

They made their way down a treacherous slope. Few springs gushed up in this dried-out country and the ground over which he would have to ride looked rugged and inhospitable. This was land which would never be conquered; wild and vast and untamable. By the time he had ridden out into the desert, with the arid dust lifting in a cloud all about him, the sun had climbed sharply up to its zenith, burning in the cloudless blue mirror of the heavens, laying a scorching touch on his neck and shoulders. It was a terrible trail, one that was scarcely ever used. He guessed that when anyone wanted to reach the mountains and the towns that lay on the far edge of the Badlands, they took the trail to the south, the hill trail. It would be longer, possibly by ten or fifteen miles, but a far easier trail on both man and horse.

He watched constantly ahead, for even here, death lay in wait at every bend of the trail. Hammerheads lay coiled in the shallow holes along the side of the trail, ready to strike out at a horse as it moved past them; and once a horse or man received a bite from one of these, he died within minutes, his body swollen, his limbs afire with agony.

In places, the trail angled down to the point where it was almost level with the bases of the towering buttes and then again, it would rise steeply, up the sides of the deep canyons, around dangerous bends so that it skirted the meandering sandstone walls of the bluffs.

The hours passed; long, tortured things. The heat head increased until he seemed to be moving through a burning, sluggish sea of air that gave him no respite. Every breath he took burned in his lungs, increased the agony in his head and although the dust kicked up by the hooves of his mount had subsided a little, the glare from the desert made it impossible to see anything clearly and had built up a sensation of nausea in his stomach. Regularly, he paused to stare into the seemingly limitless distances behind him, searching the desert for any sign of men trailing him, but as the day wore on and he saw nothing, he began to put the thought of pursuit out of his mind.

The sun was finally westering when he rode wearily on to a low shelf of ground, the only stretch that lifted above this area of the flat desert. He paused for a moment as he rolled himself a smoke, trying to put his thoughts into some kind of order. Dejection settled heavily over him as he sat the saddle thoughtfully, shading his eyes against the reddening rays of the lowering sun, gazing out over the savage wilderness that lay ahead of him, facing the inescapable fact that he was still only at the beginning of his journey, his misery and danger. In this terrible emptiness, his chances of surviving for long were low. With little water or food, a man could wander and lose himself quite easily here, until years later, another man crossing it would stumble over a pile of white, sun-bleached bones, all that remained of him. For this was country that had no need of man, did not want him, rejected him with everything at its disposal. The dunes and gulches were swarming with rattlers, hammerheads and a dozen other species of equally poisonous snake. He dismounted, stretched his stiff limbs. The terrain ahead of him was void and silent, showing no sign of movement right out to the shimmering horizon, no indication of the presence there of any other living thing.

*　*　*

It was not in Turrell to wait, but he knew that he could not continue riding through the night and expect his mount to carry him the rest of the way across the desert. He made cold camp on the ridge which was perhaps half a mile in length and lifted perhaps fifty feet above the rest of the desert. The moon came up, cold and white shortly after midnight and in his blankets, he lay on his side and watched the long shadows that lay in midnight darkness across the razor-edged gullies. The sound of horses would be muffled by the sand, he knew, even in the stillness that had dropped like a cloak about him once the sun had gone down. Unable to sleep, he rolled himself a smoke, keeping his head well down as he lit it. Even in the moonlight, a keen-eyed marksman could spot the glowing tip of a cigarette half a mile away. He smoked slowly, feeling the warmth come back into his body. In the desert, the air grew bitterly cold after dark. Finishing his smoke, he thrust the butt into the loose sand in front of him, settled back in his blankets.

He slept uneasily, waking several times, cold and miserable in the bright, clear moonlight. The steely first palings of dawn found him awake, body stiff and chilled to the bone. Swiftly, he folded up his blankets, tied them down against the saddle, let his mount eat from the coarse grass that grew in patches along the ridge, then swung up into the saddle and rode out, covering the ground with a consuming gait.

Where the pinched-down mountains reached out to the desert, with the sun high at its zenith, he splashed over a swift-moving stream, the first he had encountered since he had started out over the desert, and made good progress through the lush grasses that grew along the benchlands at the foot of the mountains.

Two hours further on and the scent of wood smoke reached him on the still air and he traced out its strengthening fragrance to discover that it originated in a small draw set among the rocks. Rounding the bend in the trail, he came out into the small clearing, saw the three men seated around the fire and reined up sharply. There were a thousand places for a man to lose himself in these mountains and one look at these men told him the type they were. Hard men, flesh burned dark by long exposure to the hot sun, scarred by trouble and maybe still looking for trouble. Along the trail, Turrell had seen many like them, restless, narrow of mind and outlook, governed by passion and greed. Such men had ridden with him further south and east before his band had been broken up.

The man nearest him moved first. He pushed himself slowly to his feet, turned and eyed Turrell sharply. The other two men fixed their gaze on him with a dead steadiness.

Turrell noticed the nearest man's hand hovering close to the gunbutt at his waist and he said quietly: 'Easy there, mister. All I want is somethin' to eat. This is one hell of a trail.'

The other hesitated, then shrugged. His hand moved away from his side, but not too far and he was clearly still suspicious. 'Step down then, stranger,' he said harshly. 'We got venison and beans.' He pointed at the fire. 'Help yourself.'

'Thanks.' Turrell stepped down from the saddle, let his horse move off into the thick grass. Squatting on his haunches, he filled the plate that one of the men thrust at him, ate the hot food slowly, savouring the taste of it. The gnawing hunger pains in his belly stilled. A mug of scalding coffee was handed to him and he washed down the meat and beans, sat back and rolled himself a smoke, aware of their glances laid on him, guessing at the thoughts that were running through their minds.

'You been long in these hills?' he asked quietly, sending a level gaze at the men around the fire.

'Sure,' said the tallest man, in a tone so false that Turrell knew he was lying, but he held the other's gaze long enough for the man to understand that he knew it to be a lie.

'See a posse ride through this way any time durin' the night?'

'We seen nobody,' grunted one of the other men, but there was a quickening note of interest in his tone. 'You ridin' from somethin'?'

'Could be.'

'Most men in these hills are.'

'I guessed that. Seems like a good place to hide out from the law.' He lit his cigarette, drew the smoke down into his lungs, aware of the close scrutiny from the three men, but giving no sign of it.

'Seems to me that you're asking a mighty lot of questions, mister,' said the tall, black-bearded man who seemed to be the leader of the group. 'Just what have you got on your mind? Where're you from?'

'Back east,' he said easily. He stared at the other through the blue smoke. In these hills there was no law except that of the gun; men had been secretly killed for a horse and whatever they carried in their saddle-bags.

'I had some men with me once,' he told them evenly, his gaze steady, his tone convincing. 'Men like I figure you are. We made a good thing near the Texas border. Trouble was, the Rangers got a little too interested in what we were doin' and moved in against us. Seems to me that this frontier here is just waitin' for somethin' like that. The law is pretty scattered and there ought to be some good pickin' to be had in these parts.'

The short man sitting opposite him lifted his head sharply. His gaze became clouded. 'There's somethin' familiar about you, mister,' he said finally. 'Could be that we've met someplace.'

'Could be,' Turrell said mildly. 'Depends where you've been.'

The other cleared his throat, spat aside, and fixed a baleful stare ahead. Then his expression cleared. 'I know you. You're Ed Turrell.'

'Turrell!' There was a sharp note of surprise in the big man's voice as he turned his head to stare at the other. 'They said you were dead. Killed by the Rangers near Tucson a year ago.'

'Then they were wrong.' Turrell grinned viciously. 'They tried to kill me. But I'm still alive and I mean to stay that way.' He could see by the looks on their faces that they were no longer suspicious.

'You mean to start again to this territory?' The short man drew in a heavy breath.

'I'd need to look the place over. Any towns in this area?'

'Triple Peaks,' broke in the big man. 'About fifteen miles to the west, over the mountains.'

'You figurin' on takin' the place?'

The other looked uncertain. Turrell gauged his moment. Around him, there was uneasiness stirring. He knew these men had visions of riding against Triple Peaks, but if they sat there much longer without reaching a decision, their resolution might dwindle. It was one thing to talk with him of moving in on this peaceful territory. It was another thing altogether to ride deliberately into trouble and the eyes of the many guns that might be ranged against them.

'I guess I've outridden that posse from Culver City,' he said with a grim smile. 'They lost my trail a long ways back. If I had some guns at my back, I reckon I could do the same here as I did near the Texas border. And this time, we could be ready for any Rangers they might send to smash us.'

71

'Sounds a decent proposition to me,' affirmed the third man, speaking for the first time. 'I like it.'

'It's a risk,' mused the small, stockily-built man from the other side of the fire. 'We've ridden into Triple Peaks and although it may be an easy town to take, there are some big men runnin' the ranches in the surroundin' territory and once they banded together against you — as they will — you'll not find it so easy.'

'They won't worry us so long as we don't bother them to start with,' Turrell said tonelessly. He turned to glance at the big man, his face hard and fixed.

'We've not been doin' so badly ourselves until now,' said the other slowly. 'What do you say, Tragge?'

The short man drew his brows together, lips set in a tight line. 'I guess so. But that don't mean to say we couldn't do a heap better if we threw in our lot with Turrell here.'

The big man fished in the cook pot for more beans, scooping them on to his plate. He chewed them thoroughly before he let them slide down his throat. With an equal slowness, he drained the mug of coffee at his side, then said heavily: 'And what guarantee do you have, Turrell, that we wouldn't run into big trouble if we backed you?'

Turrell made a toneless reply. 'You said yourself that it would be a pushover. Once we have the town all sewn up, we can start to really operate. There must be plenty of gold in the banks, or carried on the stages between here and Culver City. We could all be rich in no time. Once the goin' gets rough, we pull up stakes and ride out.'

'You figurin' on takin' on any more men?'

Turrell shrugged. 'If there are any who want to throw in their lot with us, why not? The bigger we are, the less chance the law has of stoppin' us.'

'You make it all sound so easy,' said Tragge. His gaze flicked over Turrell's face, then on to the other two men. 'Kreb and Dufray here have always been a little wary of strangers. But I vote we fall in with your plan.'

'Me, I think about this thing,' said Kreb tautly. 'I've heard about you, Turrell. You got away by the skin of your teeth when the Rangers closed in on you and left the rest of your men to die. How'd we know that the same thing won't happen again and — '

He broke off suddenly as he found himself staring down the black hole of the Colt that was lined up on his chest, Turrell's finger hard and white-knuckled on the trigger. The outlaw's lips were drawn back in a vicious, animal-like snarl. 'I don't want to kill you, Kreb,' he said thinly, speaking through tightly-clenched teeth. 'But I will if you don't take that back right now.'

For a long moment, there was a tense silence around the crackling log fire. Tension hung in the still air. Eyes were bright with challenge. The gun barrel laid on the big man's chest was stone still, steady. There was no sense in trying to gamble, although the thought of it lived for a second in the big man's eyes. Then he shrugged his shoulders slowly, let his spread-fingered hands droop and move away from his sides.

'All right, Turrell, I'm sorry,' he muttered gruflly. 'But you got to admit that it seems funny. We got to look after our own interests. We got a good thing here and it would be stupid to throw it all away and maybe our lives as well, followin' you.'

Turrell paused for a few moments longer, then thrust the gun back into leather. There had been no visible movement when he had drawn the gun and it was obvious that the three men had been virtually mesmerised by the speed of his draw. Maybe, he mused inwardly, it was this that had made them change their minds, for Dufray said smoothly: 'Ain't no point in flyin' off the handle half-cocked, Turrell. We like your plan, but we'd like to know just a little more about it.'

'Very well. Nobody knows me in this

town. I'll ride in tomorrow, look the place over. I want you to stay here for a couple of days and then ride down into Triple Peaks. By that time, we'll be ready to take over the place.'

3

Gun Rage

The long valley lay deathly hushed in the hot sun as Turrell rode down from the low foothills. It was a strangely menacing hush that began to work on him as he lifted himself up in the saddle and peered through the shimmering heat haze to where the town of Triple Peaks lay nestled close to the far horizon. A mile further along the trail which was wide and stony here, he came across a bent wooden sign that pointed in the direction in which he was travelling. It bore the simple legend: Triple Peaks.

Lifting his head from his perusal of it, he felt a faint smile form on his dust-streaked face. Off in the distance, just beyond the vague dark smudge of shadow that was the town itself, he saw the characteristic mountain chain at the back of it. Even where he was, some ten miles distant, he could make out the three sky-rearing peaks that had evidently given the town its name.

He saw no sign of life as he allowed his mount to make its own pace along the dusty trail. He was in no hurry now that his destination was in sight, perhaps three hours or so away. He should reach it before high noon and when he rounded a bend in the road and came within sight of the creek that bubbled down from somewhere in the mountains he had left at dawn, he let his mount wander with the reins trailing, giving it an opportunity to blow and drink its fill from the stream. He was a trifle bothered by the gnawing hunger pains in his stomach but this was of little inconvenience to him and he had already decided that he would eat once he got to Triple Peaks. It would give him an opportunity to learn something about the town.

Where the creek suddenly veered to

the south, cutting across the trail, he rode clear of the vegetation that grew along its banks, rode out into the hot sunlight. He had removed the bandage from around his head earlier that morning before riding out of the small camp in the hills and he could now touch the bruised flesh with his fingers without wincing every time that he did so. That doctor in the town had certainly known his business, he mused. But he was still worried about his eye. It was now virtually impossible for him to see anything clearly out of it. Only vague, blurred shapes that twisted and wavered in front of him.

Pushing on into Triple Peaks, he rode into the outskirts three hours later. It was a bigger town than he had thought and for a moment, he doubted what those three men had told him of this place. It did not look as though it would be a pushover. There was sure to be law and order here, otherwise it would never have grown to this size, never have become so obviously prosperous.

Still, one could never tell by first impressions. It was possible that there had been law and order here for so long that the townsfolk had grown used to it and would lack the ability to act swiftly when anything threatened their security.

Situated almost at the very end of the main street running through the town was a large saloon, with a hotel standing next to it. Evidently it had been decided that the best place for business was where men entered or left the town. He let his gaze drift over them, then continued on down the street, gaze flicking from right to left. In the stifling heat of high noon, there were few folk out on the street. Several men lounged in rockers on the boardwalk, seated in the shade, legs thrust out in front of them, their hats pulled down over their eyes. A few watched him as he rode by and he was acutely aware of their glance on him, knew they were appraising him, trying to guess why he was there and what sort of man he was.

Most of them, he knew, were just idlers. They might be curious for a little while, but then they would forget him. But here and there, he noticed, were others who took a more serious interest in him. In front of the sheriff's office stood a couple of men, guns slung low at their hips. Lean, hard men, with eyes that missed nothing. As he rode by, giving no sign that he knew he was being so closely scrutinised, the door of the office opened and a tall, broad-shouldered man stepped out on to the boardwalk. The star on his shirt glittered brilliantly in the flooding sunlight.

Riding on to the livery stables, he got down from the saddle, looped the reins over the horse's neck and led it towards the darkened interior. A couple of men leaning against one of the posts turned idly and after a pause, one of them took a piece of wood from between his teeth and ambled over to him.

Turrell said quietly: 'Reckon you'd

better cool him off. It's hellish hot out beyond town.'

'Been ridin' long, mister?'

'Made camp up in the hills back east. Didn't have much choice after ridin' across that desert beyond.' He handed the reins to the other. 'Where's the best place to eat in town?'

The liveryman eyed him sharply for a moment, then turned to his companion leaning against the upright. 'Hey, Joe. Take him over to Ah Fong's.'

The other man pushed himself away from the upright, stepped forward. He jerked his head towards the far side of the street. 'This way, mister,' he said tersely.

Turrell fell into step beside the other, his spurs raking tiny eddies of dust from the street. The other led him along the boardwalk for a little way, then paused, pushed open a door and said: 'In here.'

Turrell appraised him with a cool stare, then stepped inside. There the smell of hot, curried food in the air, bringing a stab of pain to the sides of his jaws. The man at his back sang out: 'Got a customer for you, Ah Fong.'

A movement behind the counter and a short statured Chinese came into view. He nodded his head, pointed to one of the tables. 'Please sit down,' he said in a high-pitched sing-song tone. 'I get you dinner.'

'Thanks.' Turrell found himself a table, sank down gratefully into the chair. The man who had brought him across said: 'Ah Fong will get you what you want. If you're figurin' on stayin' in town, I'd suggest that you check with the sheriff first. Jessup usually likes to know who's in town.'

'I'll pay him a visit as soon as I've finished eatin',' Turrell said.

The other hesitated for a moment, continued to stare down at him, then dropped his gaze, turned swiftly on his heel and walked out. Through the nearby window, Turrell saw him making his way across the street, back to his post at the livery stables, shaking his head a little as he went. Then he put all thought of the other out of his mind. Such men as Joe were of no significance as far as he was concerned. But this sheriff, Jessup, might be a different kind of animal altogether. Still, he had a couple of days to find out just how things were in Triple Peaks before those three men rode into town.

★   ★   ★

'Glad you called in to see me, Mr Smith.' Brad Jessup stared directly at Turrell, as the other sat in the chair in front of his desk an hour later. 'We welcome strangers here so long as they stay within the law. We have a good town and a decent community in Triple Peaks and we aim to keep it that way.'

'I guess you could call yourselves very fortunate then,' Turrell said. If the other felt any surprise at a man called Smith riding into town like this, he evinced no evidence of it, but continued to sit back in his chair, watching him closely, but not too obviously.

'Well . . . there is a little trouble occasionally whenever some of the Bar X boys ride into town. That's the biggest spread in these parts and they do reckon that they own the place. Mostly it's nothin' more'n high spirits, but I've been forced to lock one or two of 'em up at times and Clem Fenton don't like that. Still, there's been no open war between the cattlemen and the townsfolk so far. But I always take the opportunity of checkin' out everybody who rides into town. Just to be sure they ain't here to start trouble.'

'I understand, Sheriff.'

There was a pause, then Jessup said quietly. 'Just why are you here, Mr Smith? Ridin' through, or have you got somethin' in mind?'

'Depends, Sheriff. If I like the look of the place, I might decide to stay, I've got a little money. Might buy myself a plot of land if there is any goin' for sale. This looks like a prosperous community. Could be a good place in which to invest a little money. Reckon a man gets tired of ridin' around the country with no place to set down his roots.'

Jessup shrugged, pursed his lips. 'I don't know much about whether there's any land for sale. Reckon that Wayne Thorpe is your man for that. He's the lawyer here.' He spread his hands wide. 'It might not be a bad idea to have a talk with him anyway. It's some time since we had any real trouble in Triple Peaks.' He wrinkled his brow in thought, then went on: 'Nearly a year ago, I reckon. A couple of *hombres* rode into town and put up at the hotel along the street. Two more rode in early the next morning and joined forces with 'em. Then the four rode into the middle of town, tried to hold up the bank there. They managed to get inside and hold up the three clerks, but by the time they had the money in their saddlebags and came out, we were waitin' for 'em. Three were shot dead as they tried to ride out of town with their loot. The fourth got clear, but we ran him down in the hills and brought him back for trial. We strung him up from the big cottonwood in the square outside the next morning after he'd been tried.'

The other's voice was toneless, without expression, but Turrell knew that he was warning him that even here in Triple Peaks, they were ready to shoot it out with any outlaws who thought the place was an easy take.

'Guess outlaws steer clear of this town,' Turrell remarked, sitting forward in his chair.

'There are a few still in the hills to the east. Those hills are ten miles long and as wide. It would take an eternity to try to flush 'em out of there. But so long as they stay there, they don't worry me.'

Turrell nodded comprehension. 'You don't anticipate any trouble then, I take it.'

'None at all,' said the other easily. 'I reckon you'll be quite safe to invest your money here, Mr Smith. If you find any trouble, drop in and let me know and I'll do what I can to straighten it all out.'

'Thanks, I'll do that, Sheriff.'

★　★　★

Carefully, Turrell adjusted the patch over his left eye. It felt strange, but it had the advantage of altering his appearance sufficiently to make it difficult for anybody to recognize him from any of the posters that might be around with his picture on them. Getting to his feet he walked over to the window of his room in the hotel. It was on the top floor and beyond the glass, Triple Peaks lay smothered in the depthless mantle of night, moon-shadows lying across the street and in the distance, just visible where the moonlight painted the rocks with a pale glow, were the tall mountains on the skyline. Kreb and the others would have left them by now. At dawn, he expected them in town. During the past two days, he had moved freely in Triple Peaks, had watched and picked up all he could of the place. Now he knew the lay out of the only bank in town, the strength of the law, and also of the long-standing feud between the Bar X cattlemen and the town. This, he reckoned, was something he might eventually turn to his advantage. But the time for that lay somewhere in the future. Before then, he would lay his plans for robbing the stage that brought the payroll for the miners that worked in the hills around the town; and once that was carried out successfully, then they would turn their attention to the bank itself. Here, the experience he had had during those days along the border with Texas would be extremely useful.

He shifted position, moved a little closer to the window, not too close, for he wished to see but not to be seen. The terrain around this town was a hundred miles of nothing. There was desert to the east with scarcely any water and only the arid sand that stretched away to the inhospitable mountains; and beyond them, more desert. To the west, the country was a little better, open rangeland where it was possible to raise cattle, the long-horned ornery beasts that could live where other cattle would have starved. He made himself a smoke, stuck it unlit between his lips and stood with his shoulders leaning against the wall. Triple Peaks was not a beautiful town, he decided, even though it did have this air of prosperity about it that he had noticed instantly. Like so many of these frontier towns that had been thrown up in a hurry and in a completely haphazard manner, as if the builders had had no time at all to make plans, and had been forced to make everything completely functional, without an eye to beauty, it lacked any warmth in the stark outlines of the buildings that had been thrown up on either side of the wide road. Square, weathered and mostly unpainted, the buildings looked gloomy in the moon-light. Shielding his face with his hands, he struck a match and lit the cigarette, dragging the smoke down into his lungs. He let the smoke out slowly through his nostrils, continued to watch the street outside. Far off, out over the desertlands to the east, there were clouds gathering over the mountains and even as he watched, he saw the sharp fork-tongued flicker of lightning sparking across the heavens. The first cloudy forerunners of the coming storm drifted across the face of the moon, passed over it, followed by a clear space in which moon and stars seemed to glisten more brightly than before as if the cloud had washed them clean. Another fork of lightning and by its steely glare he saw the man who rode out of the shadows further along the street. Pressing himself back against the wall, he saw the other lift his head and stare up at the hotel for a moment as he walked his mount by in the centre of the wide street. It was the sheriff. Turrell recognized him at once. Now where was the other going at this time of night and with a storm brewing out there. Had the other become suspicious of something? Was he riding out to check the trail leading into town? For a moment a hundred burning questions ran in riotous chaos through Turrell's mind, then he suppressed them abruptly. There could easily be some quite simple explanation for the other's nocturnal wandering. It would not do to start jumping to conclusions like this. He had done nothing whatever to give the other cause for suspicion. During the whole of the two days he had carefully given the impression that he was a model citizen. His talk with the lawyer had proved more fruitful than he had thought. From him, he had learned that Triple Peaks would soon be expanding. Silver had been found in the hills to the south-west and once the news spread, there was every chance of the town growing swiftly. Thorpe had been confident that it would never become a ghost town as so many places had when gold or silver had been found, and then the strikes worked out.

The other had also let fall several hints that the feud between the Bar X and the town went deeper than Jessup had indicated. The place was almost on the point of open range war at the moment, an uneasy peace brooded over the area. Everything seemed right for a band of ruthless men to move in and take everything in front of them.

He finished the cigarette, stubbed it out in the tray on the small table, moved position slightly and tried to see along the street. But it was quiet now and there was no sign of Jessup. The other had vanished somewhere in the shadows.

Well, he told himself, within the next few days, Triple Peaks would suddenly discover that trouble had arrived there in a big way. How the townsfolk would react to the situation was something he was not sure of. The thought brought a little smile to his lips. Then he went back to the bed, stretched himself out on it, relaxing every muscle in his body.

It was good to be able to lie like this after all those weary days on the trail. He let his lids fully down and after what seemed no more than a moment but which was actually several hours, he opened them again, awake with the pale light of dawn streaming in through the window. Pulling on his jacket, he tightened his gunbelt around his middle, checked that the cylinders of the twin Colts were loaded, then jammed his hat on top of his head, stepped out into the corridor, locking his door behind him. A sleepy clerk behind the desk, taking the key from him, said: 'You goin' out before breakfast, Mr Smith? Won't be ready for another hour or so.'

'That's right. Don't save any for me. I may be gone all mornin'.'

'Sure thing,' muttered the other. There was a puzzled frown on his face as he sat down in his chair again, tilting it away from the desk with his legs braced out in front of him.

Outside in the street, he stood on the

boardwalk and looked about him in both directions. The air that sighed along the street still bore the bitter chill of the night on its breath and he pulled the collar of his coat higher around his neck, shivering a little. The street was empty as far as he could see up and down it. Stepping down into the dust, he began to walk slowly in the direction of the livery stables, then paused as two riders came around the corner of one of the narrower side streets, turned into the main street and moved their mounts in his direction. He hesitated for a moment, then quickened his pace as he recognized Kreb and Dufray.

The two men reined up as he came alongside them. He said tightly: 'Where is Tragge? What happened to him? I thought the three of you were to be here at first light.'

'Relax, Turrell,' said Kreb harshly. 'He's here. He's checkin' on the way station. Ain't no sense holdin' up that stage unless we know what's in the strong box.'

Turrell let his breath go in small pinches through his nostrils, nodded slowly. 'Sure. Guess bein' here all this time, tryin' to work things out has made me a little edgy.'

A moment later, Tragge came riding around the corner. He reined up as he saw the others, said sharply: 'They're loading up now at the way station. The strongbox went aboard while I was there. No doubt about what's in it.'

'Gold?' said Dufray tightly.

Tragge nodded. 'They're takin' three passengers and a man ridin' shotgun.'

'We can take care of him all right,' Turrell said. He threw a quick glance over his shoulder in the direction of the sheriff's office. 'But I reckon we'd better ride out of town before we attract any attention.'

* * *

They rode off the trail half an hour later, cut up into the scattered boulders which overlooked it, forming a wide ledge, from where it would be possible to see for several miles, but without being seen themselves from below. It was now past dawn and the sun had lifted clear of the horizon, was throwing long shadows across the trail where it narrowed slightly at this point, and here the stage would have to climb up over the ridge through what was virtually a pass in the rocks. It was undoubtedly the best place along the whole of the trail between Triple Peaks and the mountains for a hold-up; and because of this fact, the men accompanying the stage would be more wary at this point than anywhere else. But to Turrell's mind, this was more than outweighed by the advantages of the position.

'Guess we can sit it out and wait for a while,' Turrell said, getting down from his mount. 'That stage won't be here yet. We got plenty of time to get ready for it.'

The rocks that jutted up from the ground all about them were clean and clear in the morning light, but the floor of the valley that stretched away to their left was still in deep shadow. Turrell could hear the shrill cries of the birds in the distance where a small clump of trees sprouted from the arid earth. The rocks beneath him were cold and hard and he thought to himself, feeling a little of the dampness of the early morning mist rise about him and the cool early morning stillness of the valley: As soon as the sun has lifted to its zenith, enough to warm the rocks, this will be over and they would have struck the first blow on their way to taking over this territory.

At that same moment, five miles away to the west, Wayne Thorpe leaned his back against the seat of the rattling stage and tried to make himself comfortable. It would be a long ride out to Culver City and once the sun rose and the heat head increased its piled-up intensity, things were going to be even worse. The springs of the coach creaked ominously as they swayed from side to side of the trail and he could hear the driver, cracking the long whip and yelling at the horses as they began a long pull up a steep incline.

From beneath lowered lids he eyed the other two passengers seated opposite him. He knew them both vaguely. Carnford, a nervous little man whose adam's apple bobbed up and down in his skinny throat every time there was an untoward sound outside. Clearly he was expecting the stage to be held up at any moment, in spite of the fact that it had made this run every other day for the past year without any trouble. Jordan, broad, red-faced, was asleep, his head lolling against the corner of the coach, his breathing harsh and stertorous.

Carnford dug into his pocket and pulled out a large gold watch, stared down at it for a long moment before thrusting it back. He lifted his gaze and stared across at Thorpe. 'We seem to be making excellent time, Wayne,' he said softly. 'Do you often travel with the stage?'

Thorpe recognized that the other was seeking assurance in opening this conversation. He shrugged. 'Quite often.'

Carnford sat very still for a long while, glancing through the open window near him. Without looking back, he said: 'This is the first time for me in almost a year. It seems such a long way and there could be trouble before we hit the desert.'

'What kind of trouble are you anticipating, Mr Carnford?'

'Well, it could be anything, couldn't it? There are still outlaws in those hills yonder.' He inclined his head as he spoke towards the towering hills that had just drifted into view as the trail turned sharply to the right. 'I reckon it's no secret what we're carrying in the strongbox on this trip. They'd do anything to get their hands on that.'

'There's a guard riding shotgun,' Thorpe pointed out.

'Sure, one man against how many?' He rubbed his chin nervously with his fingers. 'Maybe I'm talking foolishly.

But it's difficult not to think of this right now.'

'Guess it would be better if you could sleep like Jordan here. Nothing seems to bother him.'

Thorpe glanced out of the window. They were crossing some barren country now and the dust, kicked up by the flying hooves of the horses, hung around them in a yellow cloud, settling everywhere. Maybe once they got the railroad through to Triple Peaks, they could make the journey in comfort, without being forced to suffer the blistering heat, the flies and the dust. Gently, he let his hand fall to the pocket of his coat, felt the comforting weight of the Derringer there. In spite of himself, Carnford's talk had had an effect on him, had made him feel a trifle nervous. He knew this trail well, knew that less than three miles ahead, they had to ride through that narrow canyon with the rocks piled high on either side. There, the trail twisted sharply and it was impossible to drive the horses through it at any speed. If there were any outlaws waiting to get their hands on the gold they were carrying in the strongbox, that was undoubtedly where they would be lying in wait.

His thoughts went on ahead as he sat there, peering through the window of the stage as it swayed precariously around a bend in the trail. He could imagine the news of the gold getting around Triple Peaks. And news like that had a way of travelling fast and reaching the wrong ears in spite of attempts to keep it a secret. He freed himself from his speculations though; they were probably not pertinent anyway. Vaguely, he could hear the driver and the guard talking between themselves on top of the stage and the continual thunder of hooves on the hard ground.

The minutes passed slowly. The glare of sunlight, striking the rocks, reflected back at every turn, a continual glare that acted with the growing heat to make them more uncomfortable. They ran down a narrow incline. On either side, rock walls began to lift, breaking now and again, but growing more solid as they progressed. They were entering the pass through the rocks. Leaning sideways a little, he kept a hawk-eyed watch on the rocks. Dimly, he heard the driver urging the horses on. Then there came the sudden sharp bark of a rifle from almost directly ahead of them, the evil, shrill whine of the slug as it spun in murderous ricochet off the rocks. There came a harsh shout. The guard seated on the box fired once, then uttered a low grunt. Out of the corner of his vision, Thorpe saw him slide sideways and crash on to the rocks, his body rolling over and over down the slope as the startled horses continued to plunge forward.

'Hold it there, driver, or you're a dead man,' yelled a raucous voice from somewhere among the rocks.

For a moment, Thorpe thought that the driver intended to ignore the warning, to slash at the horses with the whip and drive them on, hoping to run the gauntlet of gunfire. Then there came the squeal of brakes being applied, the harsh scrape of the wheels on the dirt. Stones flung up by the horses' hooves struck the side of the door.

Ignoring the danger, Thorpe pulled the Derringer from his pocket, thrust his head through the window, leaning out as far as possible. Sunlight, striking down through the narrow pass, half blinded him so that it was almost impossible for him to make out anything. Then he saw the weaving pattern of a moving man among the rocks, a man who had stepped out of cover and was advancing down the slope, holding a rifle in his hands.

'Don't be a goddamned fool,' fussed Carnford from the other corner of the stage. 'If you pull a gun on them, they'll kill us all. I'm prepared to let 'em have any valuables I'm carrying so long as they leave me be.'

Thorpe drew back his lips tightly

across his teeth. He levelled the small pistol on the man's chest, finger tightening on the trigger. Then he jerked his arm up savagely, his numbed fingers dropping the Derringer on to the rocks outside the stage as it slowed to a halt. A sharp gasp of agony broke from his lips as something scorched along his arm. He felt the warm trickle of blood oozing from the wound, was only vaguely aware of the shot that had been fired from somewhere nearer at hand.

'Don't try any heroics, mister,' snarled a voice. 'Now get out of there and keep your hands where we can see 'em.'

From the edge of his vision, Thorpe saw another shape rising up from the jumbled boulders. The outlaw came forward, a neckpiece wrapped tightly over the lower half of his face. He grasped a Colt in his right hand, the faint wisp of smoke still curling from the end of the barrel.

Clutching at the stage door with his

good hand, Thorpe climbed down and stood looking about him with a narrowing concentration. He did not recognize any of the four men who came forward now, but with the neckpieces pulled down over their faces, that was not surprising. It was not until he stared at the fourth man standing near the horses that he felt there was something oddly familiar about him, though what it was he could not quite fathom.

'Now this ain't goin' to take long, gents,' said the tallest man. He motioned with his Colt to the driver who sat with his hands raised on the stage box.

'Toss down that strongbox and be quick about it.'

'Ain't nothin' in there that will pay for holdin' up the stage,' grunted the other hoarsely.

'We'll be the best judge of that,' snapped the man near the horses. 'Just throw it down. Hurry!'

The driver complied reluctantly. The

strongbox hit the ground with a dull thump, rolled over once, then came to a standstill in the dust near the big man. He bent, caught it up and carried it over to the rocks. 'Reckon we'd better take a look inside anyway.' Pointing his revolver at the box, he fired twice. The heavy slugs tore the hasp of the lock away and he bent on one knee, throwing back the lid.

'Just like we figured,' he said, with a note of rising excitement in his voice. 'Piled high with gold. Reckon there must be close on five thousand dollars worth here. Not a bad haul.'

While he had been examining the strongbox the other three men had kept everyone covered with their guns. Now the man with the patch over his left eye moved away from the horses, stepped across to the open box and glanced inside. He nodded his head, satisfied. 'I guess we may as well relieve the passengers of anything they may have. All contributions will be most welcome.'

'You'll never get away with this, whoever you are,' said Carnford, plucking up courage. He sounded righteously indignant.

The small man nearby thrust the end of his gun barrel into the other's ribs. Carnford's face turned white as the blood drained from it and he doubled up in agony, knees buckling. He would have fallen had the other not reached out, gripped him by the shirt front, twisting the material into a tight ball in his fist, and holding him up.

'We're doin' it,' he said thickly. 'Now stand back against the stage and keep your hands lifted.'

Somehow, Carnford complied with the order. His features were still ashen, contorted by the force of the vicious blow to the pit of the stomach. He made no further protest as the other went through his pockets, ripped the gold watch away from his buttonhole with a sharp tug that tore through the cloth. He removed the other's wallet, then walked in no hurry towards Thorpe.

'You figurin' on askin' for more trouble, mister?' he sneered.

'No,' said Thorpe evenly. He was acutely aware of the pain lancing through his arm and of the blood soaking through the cloth of his jacket sleeve, but he somehow managed to keep every trace of pain and emotion out of his voice. 'But I'll personally see to it that the four of you are hanged for this.'

Patch-Eye said sharply: 'Shut up, mister; and do like he tells you. If you do that, ain't nobody goin' to get hurt.'

While two men searched the passengers, the other two carried the strongbox back into the rocks to the waiting horses. Then Patch-Eye came back. He stood for a minute watching them, then said to one of the men,

'Loosen the horses and drive them off.'

Carnford started forward at that as the truth burst upon him. 'You can't do that. You can't leave us here to die of thirst.'

'Reckon then that you'd better start walkin' it back to Triple Peaks.' The other's neckpiece ruffled as though he were grinning behind it, then throwing a quick, meaningful glance at the heavens: 'Won't be long before the sun really gets up. You don't want to wander too long in the heat. A man can go mad that way.'

While he had been talking, one of the men had unhitched the horses from the stage. Lifting his gun he fired a couple of shots into the air. The startled animals raced off along the trail, dragging their harness behind them. They would keep running for several miles, thought Thorpe before they slowed up. And these men had headed them out east, so that it was out of the question to try to walk in that direction and catch them.

The men stood quietly while Patch-Eye whistled up his horse. He climbed swiftly into the saddle, wrenched the horse's head about. Spurred heels dug deeply into the animal's flanks. A leap that covered fifteen feet and he was racing back into the rocks. The rest of the men followed him and within moments the thunderous tattoo of hooves on rock had faded into the distance.

Thorpe drew up slowly, turned to look at the other men standing near him. Slowly, he grew aware of the blood that trickled down his injured arm and of the throbbing agony of it.

'How bad are you hurt, Thorpe?' asked Jordan, stepping forward. 'Think you can make it back to town?'

'I'll make it,' said the lawyer thinly. 'I'll make it, because I mean to see to it that those four men hang for what they did today. You'd better walk back and see how the guard is. Though I reckon from the way he fell that there'll be nothing we can do for him.'

'Maybe if we were to stay here in the stage somebody would come along and then fetch help from town,' suggested

Carnford. He rubbed the pit of his stomach gently where the pistol barrel had been jammed into his flesh.

'That ain't likely, mister,' put in the driver. He rubbed a hand over his grizzled beard. 'Don't get many men usin' this trail in the heat of the day. And it'll be a long while before they get worried about us at the way station on the edge of the desert.' His narrowed eyes glanced up at the sun, a glaring white disc in the cloudless heavens. 'Reckon it's goin' to be as hot inside the stage as outside, once the sun gets to its zenith.'

'You're right,' said Thorpe. 'We have to start walking. We've got no other choice. You got any water on the stage?'

'Some,' muttered the other. He hauled himself up on to the tongue of the coach, came down a moment later with two canteens slung over his shoulder. 'I always carry these with me. Never know when they'll come in handy crossin' that hell country yonder.' He jerked a thumb in the direction of the desert that lay beyond the range of hills on the horizon. 'Once threw a wheel there and damned near died. Make sure that never happens again.'

Jordan came back along the trail. 'The guard's dead,' he said dully. 'Bullet must've killed him outright. Just below the breastbone.'

'Then we'd better leave him here, send somebody back for him when we reach town. No sense in wasting time and effort trying to bury him in this ground.'

They began the long journey back to Triple Peaks. Very soon, the burning sun was upon them with its full blasting heat and it was hard to keep walking when every step sent spasms of agony through their bodies, their feet blistered by the hard, uneven ground, the dust scoring their faces and working its way between their clothing and their flesh, gumming their mouths and eyes. When a faint breeze lifted shortly after high noon, it did nothing to soften the terrible, parching heat. Rather it made things worse, for it picked up handfuls of the itching grains of sand and flung them into their faces, even when they forced themselves to walk with bowed heads.

The fifteen miles back into town took them the whole of that day, through the blistering heat of the noon and the long, drawn-out afternoon, when every breath of air that went down into tortured lungs seemed to have been drawn over some vast oven before it reached them. By the time they staggered into the outskirts of Triple Peaks, Thorpe was in a bad way. His arm seemed swollen to twice its normal size and his mind kept wandering so that it was hard for him to concentrate on what was happening. Several times he would have fallen on that terrible trail, would have lain there unable to rise had not Jordan hauled him to his feet, forcing him on.

He drew in a great sobbing breath as they walked along the main street of town, a street that now lay covered with deep shadows, with the sun touching the distant mountain crests, a blood red orb that held very little heat. There was a cooling river of air flowing along the street but Thorpe was only vaguely aware of it, scarcely knew it when men moved out from the boardwalk, clustered about them, when a couple of men ran along the street for the sheriff and another went for the doctor.

All he was aware of was the throbbing in his arm and body, a pain that pulsed with every beat of his heart and the blood-soaked sleeve of his jacket, the red stain there clotted with the yellow-white dust from the desert. As a man in a dream, he knew that men were half-carrying him into one of the buildings by the side of the street, then there was a face bending over him, a wavering grey blur that approached and receded in a curious fashion that he could not fathom. Fingers were cutting into the fabric of his sleeve with long scissors and he felt the cold touch of steel on his flesh. Then there was nothing more for a long time.

During that period, he wakened for varying lengths of time, but on each occasion, he felt it impossible to take in anything around him. It was not until almost a week later, that he wakened and looked about him with eyes that were able to take in what they saw. He felt hungry and hot, his mind a little puzzled by what he saw.

With an effort, he tried to force himself up in the bed, but a pain, lancing through his head, forced him to relax and lie down once more, a long sigh escaping from his lips. He kept his eyes open, staring up at the ceiling above him, trying to sort things out in his mind, trying to remember what had happened and how he came to be in this room, one which he did not recognize. These thoughts were still running through his mind when he heard the door of the room open and someone come in. With a wrench of neck muscles, he turned his head to look round and a voice said:

'So you're awake at last, Wayne. I never thought I'd see you pull through.'

Thorpe narrowed his eyes. For a moment, his vision seemed curiously blurred. Then he recognized the man standing beside the bed. 'Hello, Doctor,' he said, his voice sounding strained and flat so that he scarcely recognized it as his own. 'Where am I? What happened?'

Doc Wheeler smiled faintly, seated himself in the chair near the bed and felt for Thorpe's pulse. 'You've been very ill, Wayne,' he said quietly. 'In fact, there were times when I never thought you'd recover. That bullet in your arm must have set up some form of poisoning and that trek here was more than enough to half kill you. If you hadn't the constitution of a horse, you'd be dead by now, in spite of my expert doctoring.'

Turning his head, Thorpe glanced at his arm. There was a bandage around it and it felt stiff whenever he tried to move it. But his mind was clear now and gradually, memory returned. At first, only in little snatches, but then forming a recognizable picture.

He rubbed a hand over his forehead. 'I remember now. The stage was held up by four masked men. Did you get them?'

Wheeler shook his head. 'They lit out for the mountains apparently. There was no chance of finding them there, although Jessup took out a posse the same night that you arrived back in town.' His face remained serious as he spoke and Thorpe watched him closely for a moment before speaking.

'Seems to me you've got something else on your mind, Doc. What is it?'

'You know how long you've been unconscious, Wayne?'

'A couple of days judging by how hungry I feel.'

'Just over a week,' said the other tightly. 'And in that time, those outlaws have struck again, not once, but three times. They hit the bank in Culver City, got away with nearly ten thousand dollars. They attacked the pay office of

118

the Mining Company and they robbed one of the stores here in Triple Peaks.'

Thorpe lay for several moments, trying to digest this news. It was hard to believe. For a long time now, they had lived without trouble in this part of the territory. True, they had long known that there were outlaws in the hills to the east, but until now those men had made no attempt to attack the town. They had seemed content to stay there, out of reach of the law. Now they had been formed into an outlaw band by someone and their reign of terror had clearly begun.

'And what is Jessup doing about it?' he demanded weakly. 'Is he just sitting in his office and letting this happen?'

'Seems to me that Jessup isn't concerning himself overmuch with what's been happening,' remarked the other, with a curious tone in his voice. 'He's taken out a posse now and again, but with no success. If you ask me, he's scared of meeting up with these *hombres*.'

'That's what I figured,' said Thorpe evenly. He felt a faint chill of premonition in his mind, shivered a little. What horror was about to be let loose on the town in the near future? he wondered tensely.

It took sightly less than a week for Thorpe to be up on his feet again: Even at the end of that time, he did so in the face of opposition from the doctor. There was a subdued grimness in Triple Peaks now, a feeling that Wayne Thorpe recognized the first time he walked through the town. He recognized also the deep-seated uneasiness of the townsfolk. It was undeniably the attack on the store, more than the hold-up of the stage, which contributed most to their grimness. That, and the fact that it was becoming increasingly plain that the law, in the person of Sheriff Jessup, seemed unable to cope with the situation.

Very soon, the people of Triple Peaks would have to face up to the situation. If they had known of Thorpe's suspicions, they would have been even more apprehensive. It seemed to the lawyer that nobody had noticed that shortly before the stage had been held up, the man who had called himself Smith, had vanished from the town and had not been seen since. Whether there was any connection, he was not sure; but on the third day after he was allowed up, Wayne Thorpe went along to the telegraph office and sent off an urgent telegram.

4

Stranger in Town

From long habit, Garth Martinue rode through the blasting midday heat at a leisurely gait. When a man had long distances to cover, the slow way was the best. He had been travelling now for seven days and in all of that time, he had seen men only at a distance, as tiny clouds of yellow-white dust along the rim of the desert, clouds of dust that had seemed no bigger than a man's hand. He had received the message from Wayne Thorpe in Triple Peaks a little over eight days before. At first, he had puzzled over it, then decided to act on it, and had set out the very next day, knowing the long distance he had to cover and wondering why his old friend had sounded so urgent in the telegram.

For a moment, he straightened up in

the saddle, rubbed his face where the dust had mingled with the sweat, forming an irritating mask over his flesh. He rode with a rider's looseness about him. The clear grey eyes watching every movement in the rocks about him. There had been little to keep him company now except for the purple sand lizards and an occasional rattler coiled in a hollow among the rocks.

The single rifle shot came clear and loud in the clinging stillness, shattering the silence into screaming fragments of sound, the slowly atrophying echoes dying away among the slow-rising hills. Swiftly, instinctively, Garth swung himself around in the saddle, jerking up the reins, holding them tightly as he felt the horse start at the sudden, unexpected sound. Eyes narrowed as they searched the low hills about him, he tried to make out the direction from which the crack of the gunshot had come, but he could not. There were too many narrow canyons and bluffs close by to refract the sound and channel it into a

123

multitude of different directions. Then, abruptly, there came the sound of another shot. This time, he judged it to be a revolver shot and he gauged it to come from his right, from somewhere beyond the narrow tangle of scrub that grew along the top of the bluff above him. Swinging the horse around, he put it to the steep ascent. Hooves clawing at the loose shale and dirt underfoot, the horse began the long struggle to the top. It was hard going and Garth leaned back in the saddle to help the animal.

At length, they rode over the top of the ridge, through the sword grass and chapparal that lay in their path. Shading his eyes against the glaring sunmash, he stared ahead of him, seeking the antagonists in this gunfight. At first, he could see nothing. Then, in the shadow of one of the uprearing boulders, he caught a glimpse of the flat wagon, drawn a little to one side of the narrow twisting trail. Even as he spotted it, there came another shot, followed by more from somewhere among the boulders. Somebody was down near that wagon, firing at men up in the boulders, he decided instantly. Gigging his mount forward, he rode down the steep slope, feet thrust out straight in the stirrups, right hand jerking the long-barrelled Colt from leather, finger across the trigger.

Rounding a sharply-angled bend, he came in full view of the wagon. The horses still stood in the traces, but they were restless, champing at the bit, ready to lunge forward any second if the firing continued. There was the body of a man lying across the back of the wagon, whether he was dead or merely wounded it was impossible to tell at that distance.

Swiftly, he slid from the saddle, diving for the cover of the rocks and crouched down on his haunches, the gun levelled, seeking some target. There had to be someone near that wagon down there, he mused, although he could see no one. Unless it had been that man and the bushwhackers had finished him. He waited to see if anyone came down out of the hills to check their kill. Nothing stirred among the boulders. Garth knew that he was well screened from view by the brush that grew among the boulders.

Time moved slowly in the dusty, arid draw, but he knew that the killer's curiosity thought nothing of time and was an urgent thing. Less than thirty seconds later, his sharp-eyed gaze caught sight of the faint movement in the rocks on the far side of the trail. He lifted his head slightly, saw the man move from one concealing shadow to another as he began to work his way down the slope, angling across it slightly so as to bring himself close to the wagon. Garth's first instinct was to lift his gun and draw a bead on the other, but he knew that the distance was too great for a revolver and his rifle was still in the scabbard near the saddle on his mount. No time to go back for it. If the other continued to move forward, he would soon come within range, and before he got to the wagon. He waited with bated breath. Maybe there were other bushwhackers among those boulders, but as yet, they did not seem keen on showing themselves. Could be they were waiting to see if that hombre on the wagon was really dead, or whether he was merely playing possum, ready to open fire as soon as they showed themselves within range of his gun.

The other seemed to be a big man and he moved slowly and with great caution. He came right to the lip of the overhang less than thirty yards from the wagon, peered down at it. A moment later, so suddenly that it took Garth completely by surprise, a shot rang out and the bushwhacker dropped from sight as the slug hit close beside him, splashing powder from the rock face. So there was someone else down there at the wagon.

He leaned forward, tried to make out who it was, then caught sight of the slight figure lying behind the rear wheel. Even from that distance, he was able to see that it was a woman. The fact struck him with an almost physical violence. Edging forward, he scrambled down among the rocks. Out of the corner of his eye, he saw the other figures now, further along the trail, moving forward in an attempt to swing around the girl and take her from the rear. Sliding down on his heels in a cloud of dust and stones, he lunged to one side, loosed off a couple of shots as he came to a standstill.

One of the men, lifting himself up on to his knees to get a better shot at the girl lying behind the wagon, suddenly drew himself up on to his toes, clutching at his shoulder as he did so, dropping the gun in his fist. He fell back out of sight among the rocks. The other two men, a few yards away, turned sharply at this new menace, threw shots across the trail, then turned and fled into the rocks.

Total silence closed down. Very slowly, not sure of the welcome he would get from the girl at the wagon, he got to his feet and made his way down to the trail. From somewhere in the distance, there was the sound of horses moving off among the rocks, further back from the trail, horses being ridden hard. Clearly the bushwhackers, whoever they were, did not relish the idea of tangling with someone who could shoot as well as he could. So long as they had only a man and a girl to contend with, they were quite content to move in.

Now they were doubtless running as fast as they could and would not stop running until they were well away from this place and certain there was no pursuit. There was so great a weight of stillness lying over the area now that his own harsh breathing made a loud sound in the silence. Going down on to the trail he approached the wagon. The girl was on her feet now, facing him and she held the revolver tightly in her slim hand, the barrel pointed straight at him, her finger still on the trigger.

Deliberately, he thrust his own weapon back into its holster, held his hands well away from his sides as he continued to move forward.

'Better be careful what you do with that gun,' he said evenly. 'It might go off if you've an itchy trigger finger.'

The girl regarded him stolidly for a long moment, still wary, still unsure of him, then he saw her shoulders slump fractionally, hurried forward and caught her arm as she fell against him.

'You're all right now,' he said quickly. 'They've gone. I guess they won't be back here in a hurry. But we'd better take a look at him.' He nodded towards the man slumped over the back of the wagon. 'Who is he?'

'My father,' said the girl, her voice oddly hushed. 'I think he's — '

'I'll take a look at him.' Gently, he urged her towards the seat of the wagon, waited until she was seated, then turned his attention to the grey-haired man. Turning him over, he found the blood stain on the front of his shirt, felt for the pulse. It still beat in the other's wrist, slowly, but strongly.

Tearing the shirt aside, he noticed that the slug had torn across the man's shoulder. It had made a nasty wound, but it looked worse than it probably was and a quick examination satisfied him that the bullet had merely hit the bone a glancing blow and emerged again. At least, there was no necessity to dig for the slug, he thought gratefully.

'Is he dead?' The girl's quavering voice reached him from the front of the wagon.

'No, he's still alive. But I reckon we should get him to a doctor as soon as we can. Where's the nearest town?'

'Triple Peaks. That's where we were heading when those men jumped us. It's about fifteen miles away to the west.'

'He should make it all right. Think you can handle the horses or would you like me to drive the wagon? I can hitch my own mount behind.'

'I think I'd feel better if you'd drive,' she said in a small voice.

Whistling down his horse, he hitched

it to the back of the wagon, checked that the girl's father was lying as comfortably as possible, then climbed up on to the tongue beside her, taking the reins between his fingers.

They drove slowly along the trail, taking care not to disturb the wounded man any more than possible. Garth was not sure how badly hurt the other really was. He had, like many other men who rode the wide trails, tended broken limbs and patched up wounded men before. But the other was an old man. He could not be expected to survive a bad wound like a younger, fitter man.

'You got any idea who those dry-gulchers were?' he asked at length, glancing at the girl out of the comer of his eye.

'I'm not sure.' She sounded dubious. For a long moment, she was silent. Then she went on in a low voice: 'I'm Rosarie Glynn. My father owns one of the ranches outside of Triple Peaks. We left Culver City the day before yester-day on our way back. There's been talk of outlaws operating in the hills on the edge of the desert. They've attacked a couple of banks, held up the stages along this trail, killed almost a dozen men since they began operating about a month ago. I think it must have been them. They've been getting stronger and more audacious all the time. If they dare to ride into a town like Triple Peaks in broad daylight and rob one of the stores there, then they wouldn't think twice about holding up a wagon along the trail.'

Garth nodded his head slowly. It made sense. But why were these outlaws allowed to get away with it? Was the sheriff in Triple Peaks working in cahoots with them? It was a possibility. He had met up with several crooked sheriffs in the past, knew them for the lowest form of being to walk the earth. Any man who hid behind a law badge and worked with crooks was lower than a rattler's belly.

'Who's the law in Triple Peaks?' he inquired.

The girl eyed him sharply for a moment, then shrugged her slim shoulders. 'Sheriff Jessup.'

'You know what sort of a man he is?' The meaning behind Garth's question was perfectly obvious to the girl. The look on her face told him so.

'If you mean, is he working for these outlaws, then the answer is no. I don't believe he is.'

'Yet he doesn't seem to be doing anything to stop them.'

'No,' she mused. 'But I think it's simply that he isn't cut out to be a lawman. This is the first time that anything like this has happened in Triple Peaks for more than a year, before he became sheriff. I know he declined the offer of the job when they first made it. But since there was nobody else around to take it on, he eventually accepted.'

'I see.' Garth tried to keep the grimness out of his voice. A weak-kneed man for sheriff. No wonder these outlaws found it so easy to take over the town and operate in this territory. And once they had a start, unmolested by the law, within a little while they would grow too strong for it, when the time came for someone to try to move against them. That was undoubtedly the big danger. Outlawry was a disease that struck at these frontier towns and territories. A canker that infected the area, prevented them from growing as they ought to grow. Unless they were eradicated at the source, before they had a chance to increase in size, it was the devil's own job to smash the gangs. Their weapons were fear and sudden, unexpected death. No man could really be safe from them. Weak-willed men fell in with them rather than try to face up to them; and even if a man did come along who dared to stand up to them, it was difficult for him to get guns to back up his play.

He thought of the piece of paper in his pocket, bearing the message sent by Wayne Thorpe. Now, he was beginning to see things a little more clearly, could understand the urgency behind that message. He wondered though, whether the outlaws had access to the telegraph office. If they had, and it was more than likely, then they would know of his impending arrival in Triple Peaks and his task and the danger associated with it, would be multiplied tenfold.

Two hours further on, they came within sight of the town. It lay slumbering in the heat haze of afternoon, a town that seemed to be without any sounds at all. It was much too quiet, Garth decided as he drove the wagon along the dusty river of the main street, the sound of the rattling wheels thrown back at them from the wooden buildings on either side.

He halted the wagon in front of the sheriff's office. The door opened and a big, broad-shouldered man came out, paused for a moment on the edge of the plankwalk, then hurried down into the street and came towards them, throwing a quick, suspicious glance at Garth and then switching his gaze to the man laid out on the back of the wagon.

'What happened to your father, Rosarie?' he said anxiously.

'We ran into trouble about fifteen miles out, Sheriff,' said the girl, climbing down from the tongue of the wagon. She shook her head a little so that the long, corn-coloured curls swung from side to side, catching the last light of the sun, forming a burnished halo about her head. 'Outlaws. I don't know how many there were, but we would both have been killed if it hadn't been for this stranger here.'

The sheriff bent over the girl's father, then straightened, called to one of the small knot of men gathered on the sidewalk. 'Get Doc Wheeler. Hurry. Clem has been hurt bad.'

One of the men hurried away, came back a little while later with an oldish man, his hair greying at the temples. He carried a black bag with him, set it down on the corner of the wagon and bent over the wounded man. While he made his examination, the sheriff walked over to where Garth stood near the horses. His eyes were a shade hard as he said: 'You're a stranger in these parts, aren't you, mister?'

'That's right,' replied Garth easily. 'The name is Martinue — Garth Martinue.'

'Mind if I ask you why you're here in Triple Peaks?'

'I figure that must be pretty obvious. I drove this young lady and her father here to get help. I couldn't very well leave them stranded out there on the trail. Those outlaws could've doubled back and finished them off.'

'That don't answer my question, Mr Martinue. I get the feelin' that you were headed here in the first place before you met up with Rosarie Glynn and her father.'

'That could well be.' Garth spoke easily, his tone still pleasant, but a little of the steel beneath the surface was beginning to show through. 'But if it is, I reckon it's my own business.'

'That's as maybe,' retorted the other. His face grew hard. 'But as sheriff here, it's my duty to make sure that there's no trouble and — '

'It would seem to me from what I've heard on the way here that there's trouble aplenty in Triple Peaks and so far nobody has done anythin' about it. If I had outlaws operatin' within a few miles of my town, I'd want to know where their hide-out was and then get a posse ready and go out after them, hunt them down.'

'You seem to know an awful lot about what's been happenin' here for somebody who's just ridden into the territory.' The look of suspicion flared up into the lawman's eyes again and he let his gaze roam over Garth's face as he stood off a few paces.

'I make it my business to know what I'm ridin' into,' Garth said softly.

'It could be that you're ridin' into a heap of trouble.' The other lifted his brows a shade. 'My advice to you is tread carefully so long as you're in town. We had a stranger ride in a few weeks ago, shortly before all this trouble broke out. Ain't nobody seen him since.'

'I'll watch out for myself,' Garth said. He turned to where the doctor had straightened up after finishing his examination. 'How is he, Doc?'

'He'll live. It's a bad flesh wound and he's lost a lot of blood. Having to bring him here in the wagon all that way didn't help none. Still, I reckon he ought to be up on his feet in a few weeks as good as new. That shoulder of his is going to be a mite stiff from now on, but it oughtn't to worry him too much.' Wheeler turned to a couple of the men standing near the wagon. 'Lift him down, boys, and carry him along to the surgery. And be careful how you handle him. No sudden movements or you could start that bleeding again.'

Two of the men stepped forward, took the wounded man by the legs and shoulders and lifted him gently from the wagon. The small, interested crowd which had gathered in the street parted to let them through and Doc Wheeler followed close on their heels, carrying his bag in his hand. He vanished into the crowd.

Garth turned to the sheriff. 'Is there anythin' more you want to ask me, Sheriff. Or can I go and fix myself up with a room at the hotel?'

Jessup turned his gaze on the other for a long moment, then shrugged. 'Just so long as you don't make any trouble, you're welcome to stay. But I'll be watchin' you until I'm sure of you.'

After the other had walked back into the sheriff's office, the girl touched Garth's arm, said in a low voice: 'Don't pay any heed to him, Garth. It's just that he's jumpy. There have been too many things happening these last few weeks and the job seems to be getting on top of him. He's ready to suspect everybody who rides into town of being in cahoots with the outlaws.'

'I understand,' Garth nodded. Going to the rear of the wagon, he unhitched his horse, led him back. 'Reckon I'll get my mount bedded down and then get myself a room in the hotel.'

'I'm sure we'll meet again, Mr Martinue,' said the girl, smiling. She held out her hand, her grip warm and friendly. 'And thank you again for what you did.'

'It weren't nothing, Miss Glynn.' He gave her a lopsided smile. After she had gone, he stood there for a further moment in the middle of the street, but his gaze was not on her retreating figure, but was fixed further in the distance, to where the darkly-hazed mountains were just visible in the deepening gloom of the approaching night and there was something of hardness and a grim determination in his gaze, a look that was almost frightening.

After he had registered in the hotel, he went up to his room on the top floor, washed the dust of the trail from his face and neck, rubbed himself down with a rough towel, then buckled on the heavy gunbelt and went downstairs into the diner. He chose a table set a little distance from the door, ordered a meal, and ate ravenously. He had eaten little since dawn that day and when he had finished his meal and drunk two cups of hot, black coffee, he found that his supper had acted as a stimulant. He turned over in his mind everything that had happened that day, particularly the information he had gleaned from the girl.

He wondered vaguely about Jessup. He had not expected him to be the kind of man he had turned out to be when he had met him face to face. He had not expected this man to be afraid of riding out after the outlaws, nor of being in league with them. Still stranger things had happened and he knew how the promise of wealth could sway a man, even a man sworn to uphold the law.

There had been something a little more definite than mere suspicion in the way the other had acted too, when they had met. It was almost, he decided, as if the other had, for some reason, decided to be openly antagonistic towards him.

Building himself a smoke, he lit the cigarette, sat back in his chair, and smoked it slowly. He had been tired when he had ridden into town. Now he felt alive, better. Shrewd lines appeared around the bridge of his nose and the corners of his eyes as he sat there and contemplated the few diners at the other tables.

When he had finished, he went along to the stables, checked on his horse, and then made his way slowly along the street, past the lighted windows, until he came to the house he was seeking. Pausing in front of the door, he stared off in both directions along the quiet street, then rapped sharply on the door with his knuckles.

It opened a moment later, and Wayne Thorpe stood there in the opening, peering out at him. For a moment, there was no recognition on the lawyer's face. Then his expression cleared, he thrust out a hand, grasped Garth's tightly, shook it, then motioned him inside, closing the door softly behind him.

'Garth! It's good to see you again. I half thought you didn't get my message.'

'Got it eight days ago.' Garth followed the other into the parlour where a lamp was burning yellowly on the table. There were wooden shutters across the windows, battened down with a stout crosspiece. 'Came here as soon as I could. I gathered from your letter that the matter was urgent, but you didn't say what it was.'

Thorpe nodded his head quickly, went over to the cupboard, came back with a bottle and two glasses. Pouring out the drinks, he handed one glass to Garth, then seated himself in the other chair, his serious face etched with shadows.

'I couldn't trust this matter to the telegraph.' He sipped his drink slowly, thoughtfully. 'I tried to make it sound as urgent as possible without actually mentioning the position, in order to whet your appetite sufficiently to get you here when I could explain things in full. When did you arrive in town?'

'A couple of hours ago.' Garth leaned back. The whiskey tasted good on his palate. 'I ran into a little trouble on the way here. Bushwhackers trying to shoot up an old man and his daughter.'

The other gave a quick, brief nod. 'Clem Glynn and Rosarie. I heard about that a little while ago. It's just something more to add to what has happened these past few weeks. When it became obvious that Jessup, the sheriff, didn't intend to do anything about it, I decided that we needed help from outside. That was why I sent for you.'

'But why me?'

'You were the only man I could think of who might be able to help us. After all, since you smashed that outlaw gang operating down near the Texas border, I figured that you had the experience for dirty work like this. I won't hide from you the fact that it is dirty work. Nobody knows where these killers came from. They just sprang up from nowhere. They held up the stage I was on and killed the guard, got away with the strongbox containing about five thousand dollars worth of gold bullion. They shot me in the arm, laid me up for a week or so. Doc Wheeler reckons I was lucky to be alive.'

'Have you got any idea where they may be hidin' out?'

'In the hills probably. You came through them on your way here, just on the edge of the desert. They're wide enough and long enough to hide a hundred outlaws and full of trails that nobody knows. A man could lose himself in there and it would take an army to find him.' He paused, filled their glasses once more, then went on: 'This was a decent town only a little while ago, Garth. I know that it's hard to believe that now. In fact, it's hard to believe it ever was safe for decent citizens to live in. Now we've got this blight in the territory. It's like some disease that has to be cut out before it gets a chance to spread.'

'From what I've already been able to learn, it seems that it's gettin' too late for that. When they can ride into a town in broad daylight and rob the bank or one of the stores, then it isn't going to be easy to smash them.'

'I know. That's one of the main reasons why I sent for you. You've got to help us. I know of no one else.'

Garth could not help noticing the plea in the other's tone. He searched for his tobacco, rolled himself another smoke, struck and cupped the match to his face and drew the smoke deep into his lungs. He said slowly: 'Somehow, I've got the feeling that Jessup isn't goin' to like me diggin' into things. He made it plain when we met that he didn't like me for some reason.'

Thorpe sat back in his chair, regarded Garth seriously. 'I don't think you need to worry about Jessup. He's all talk, but he does nothing. But I would advise you to move easy around town. All strangers coming in here are watched, and watched closely. A man might be in league with the outlaws, in town to get information for another raid. This is one hell of a town now, Garth. Every time I walk down that street out yonder, I get to wondering just when everything is going to bust wide open and blow this place apart. It's like sitting on top of a goddamned powder keg with the slow fuse lit, not knowing when it's going to go off and blow us all to perdition.'

'I'll take care and walk easy.' Garth set down his glass on the table nearby. 'But don't tell Jessup who I am. It might be better if nobody but you know about me. As far as the rest of the town is concerned, I'm just another drifter riding through.'

Thorpe considered that for a moment, then shrugged his shoulders. 'If that's the way you want to play it, then naturally I'll do as you say. But I think it only fair to warn you that you might find nothing but open hostility on the part of the townsfolk here. You might not find it easy to get information from them.'

'That's a risk I'll take,' Garth said evenly.

'You're sure you want to take it?' said the other, brows drawn together in a straight line.

'That doesn't seem to be the question. It's a risk which has to be taken, I'm sure of that.'

'All right. If there is any way in which I can help, then I'll be only too willing to do so. I'm not much good with a gun now, but I reckon I can — '

'I won't need you to back me with gunplay, Wayne,' Garth said seriously. 'Rest assured about that. But if it comes to a showdown with the sheriff. I'd like to know that I've got you at the back of me.'

'Don't worry, I'll back you there,' affirmed the other. He lifted the whiskey bottle again, but Garth shook his head. 'I reckon I'll take a look around this town while it's dark,' he said quietly, getting to his feet.

'Be careful. A bullet could come from any unlighted corner,' warned the other. 'I've seen it happen so many times in my life.' He stood at the door and watched the other walk out onto the boardwalk and then stride off into the night.

5

Gunsight

With each ugly outline of the town buildings just visible in the gloom, Garth eyed the lights that showed through the windows on either side of the main street, then crossed through the burnished dust to the far side of the street. There was a huge cottonwood growing in the middle of the square where two roads intersected and a wooden bench all the way around the bottom of the thick trunk. An earthen olla hung suspended from one of the branches and he upended it and drank all of the cool water he could, slaking the thirst that was now in him.

Seating himself on the bench, he waited in the cool darkness, thrusting his legs forth to their full length and from time to time, he turned his head slowly to peer in both directions along the streets that radiated away from this point. It came to him that a man could sit here and see almost everything that went on in the streets of Triple Peaks.

Five minutes after he had seated himself there, the door of the sheriff's office opened, the burly figure of Sheriff Jessup appeared for a moment in the swathe of light, then the light went out, the door was locked and Jessup strode purposefully across the street and into the saloon on the opposite side. He did not look aside towards the man seated on the bench.

Less than two minutes after the sheriff had vanished, a man came out of the saloon, peered around him cautiously for a long moment, then hurried away into the darkness. He carried something small and white in his hand. Leaning forward, Garth saw that the other had paused in front of the telegraph office. There was still a lamp burning there and Garth guessed that the night man was on duty. The man was lost to Garth's gaze for less than five minutes, then he reappeared, trotted quickly back to the saloon and went inside. Garth rubbed his chin thoughtfully. The sequence of events he had just witnessed began to add up to something definite in his mind. It seemed evident that Jessup was unsure about him, wanted to know a lot more than he did already, so he had sent this man to send a wire. Maybe it had been to the sheriff in Culver City, asking if he had anything on a man who called himself Garth Martinue.

Had the other anything on his mind other than suspicions? For Garth was not a wanted man and there was no reason why Jessup should imagine he was. He rose slowly to his feet, drawing himself up to his full height. Slowly too, he made his way along the boardwalk, heading for the saloon on the very edge of town, which he had noticed when he had ridden in with Rosarie Glynn. He kept his hands close to the guns at his waist as he walked, aware of the hollow sound of his boots on the plankwalk. This was a town where men could turn into his enemies on a single word from many men, where he was a stranger and all strangers were looked upon as potential outlaws. He could believe that it had been a good town once, maybe not so long before; but since this band of outlaws had begun operating from this part of the territory, no man felt safe; and it was easier to shoot first and ask questions later, than to keep a possible killer in their midst.

He paused as he came alongside the telegraph office, an idea forming in his mind. Acting on impulse, he opened the door and stepped inside. The operator sat in his tilted chair, his legs on the small table in front of him, the morse key at his back. He was reading the daily newspaper, looked up over the top of it as Garth entered.

'Howdy, mister,' he said genially. There was no suspicion on his face, just an open frankness that Garth liked at once. Here, he thought, was a man who could be trusted, but it might be that his honesty could make it difficult for Garth to get any information out of him.

'Howdy. Jessup wants to know how long before you get an answer to that message?'

The other shrugged. 'Jessup's in one hell of a hurry,' he replied. 'I told Bill it would likely be near mornin' before any answer came through. Where is Jessup now?'

'Over at the saloon.'

'That's what I figured. Well, I reckon he ought to know then that Cantry, in Culver City, is probably in the same place and he won't like it if somebody goes across to drag him out just to ask if some hombre happens to be a Texas Ranger. Not that Cantry is likely to know anyway.' He grinned a little. 'Still if Jessup wants to spend his money on fool questions that ain't likely to be answered, that's all right by me. I've just got a job to do.'

'Thanks, I'll tell him to wait until

mornin'.' Garth nodded, went outside again, walked slowly to the end of the street. The news had disturbed him a little. Had Jessup been wanting to know if he was a suspected outlaw, he would have given it no other thought. But why had the other thought he might be a Texas Ranger? He was getting just a little too close to the truth to be healthy.

One thing was clear; he would have to move carefully now, what with most of the townsfolk here thinking he might be an outlaw, and Sheriff Jessup believing him to be a Ranger. This made him smile. If word got out to the outlaws in the hills they would certainly take every desperate means they could to kill him; they had to; and he knew they could make deadly enemies.

Before going into the saloon, he made a slow-swinging search of the night, saw nothing suspicious, then pushed open the batwing doors with the flat of his hands and stepped through into the noise and the light and

157

the bluehazed smoke of the saloon. It was more crowded than he had anticipated. In one corner, a small, ferret-faced man was playing a piano, evidently an instrument which had been newly imported into the town judging by the way many of the men were crowded around it. Then he noticed the woman who had walked down the stairs just before he had entered. She wore a brilliant red gown that matched the colour of her lips, and her face, which could have been soft once, now had a certain hardness to it that he recognized at once. A woman who had come out west, seeking a new life, some years back, and who had been swiftly disillusioned.

But when she began to sing, he forgot all of that. Her voice was low and warm, with a smoky quality that made everyone in the saloon quieten at once. She sang in a language he did not understand, which he guessed was French, but although he could not understand the words, the melody of the song was enough to conjure up a picture of a place where the skies were always blue, the sun warm and a woman's love lasted for ever. Where there was no poverty, no sudden, violent death, and everything was peace.

He walked slowly to the bar, stood with his elbow resting on the low rail, caught the eye of the bartender and lifted a finger. The other paused, glanced back at the woman who sang by the piano, then came over, placing a bottle and glass in front of him. Garth kept his fingers curled around the neck of the bottle as the other moved to take it away.

Filling his glass, he sipped it slowly. His dark brows drew inward and downward as he turned his head to glance at the men in the saloon. They looked the usual assortment one found in a place such as this. A few nesters by the look of their clothes, one or two cattlemen, the rest townsfolk. At the moment, all of their attention was focused on the woman who sang. They had not noticed him in their midst.

The song ended. In spite of requests to sing another song, the woman withdrew, moved back up the winding stairway and vanished from sight at the top. A beefy looking man in a gaudy waistcoat and frock-coat climbed on to the small stage near the pianist and called loudly:

'Rosie will be back in a little while, gentlemen. In the meantime, there are faro and poker games and plenty of whiskey to drink at the bar.'

Garth poured a second drink, and out of the corner of his eye, he saw the bartender, at the far end of the bar, lean forward and whisper something to a small knot of men standing there. As one man, their heads turned in his direction, their hard stares looking him up and down.

Trouble, he decided, every nerve alerted, every muscle in his body poised, ready. It was no more than he had expected.

One of the men put down his glass and moved towards Garth. He was a little shorter than Garth, but broad, stocky of shoulder and wearing a black, bristle-sharp moustache. He got directly in front of Garth as the other made a half-turn at the bar. Suspicion lay in the room which had now gone suddenly quiet. Tension held the men at the bar and the tables quiet, tight. The man at the piano, sensing trouble, struck up a jangling tune, then stopped as one of the men moved over to him, leaned on the side of the instrument and said something in a sharp undertone.

The man in front of Garth said: 'Don't you know better than to be walkin' the streets like this, mister?'

Garth gave him a level stare, meeting the other's sharp-bright gaze head on. 'Who owns the streets of this town?' he said thinly.

One of the men at the far end of the bar said loudly: 'He rode into town with Rosarie Glynn, Jeb. Brung in her father on the back of the wagon.'

'Now maybe he figures that makes him somethin' of a hero,' sneered the big man hoarsely. He stood with his hands cocked ready at his sides, hungering for a fight. 'Maybe he's strange here and don't know what's been happenin' these past few weeks. Or maybe he ain't strange at all and he knows what he's doin'.'

'Suppose you tell me what I'm doin'?' Garth said softly, very soft.

'I reckon you're here to get information for those killer friends of yours up in the hills,' said the other without hesitation. 'We know they're gettin' in somehow and it has to be from somebody in town.'

'So why should it be me?'

The other drew back his lips over his teeth in a mirthless grin. 'Easy won't do it, mister,' he snapped. 'If you came here lookin' for trouble — ' he paused and gave that idea some thought, went on: 'then I reckon that you've come to the right place.'

Garth waited, knowing that this man wanted to fight; he could see it in his stance, in the way his fingers were curled into his palms, tight-fisted. This was the identical stand, the same look that he had seen in similar circumstances several times in the past. He let his gaze wander over the other. There was a broad, red scar down the side of the man's face, whether from a bullet wound or a fist fight, it was difficult to tell. He looked strong and capable, had clearly survived much violence, most of it of his own making, and now he wanted more; a man governed and living by passion.

'I reckon you'd better back off, mister,' said Garth quietly. He let his gaze slide past the other to the small knot of men standing at the end of the bar, men too obviously interested in what was going on. His grin was tight-lipped. 'Besides, I don't like the idea of guns coverin' me.'

The big man jerked his head around, then growled: 'They won't interfere in this, mister. Shuck that gunbelt.' As he spoke, he unbuckled his own belt and tossed it across the floor until it came to rest near the bar. He started forward, flat-footed, arms swinging loosely by his sides.

There was no alternative for Garth. He recognized this at once. The man was committed and would never back down. Unbuckling the gunbelt, he let it drop about his feet, knew in a second that this was exactly what the other had been waiting for. Before he could kick the gunbelt clear, the other had leapt forward, swinging in a couple of bone-crushing blows to the body. Only Garth's experience of dirty fighters saved him in that instant. He twisted instinctively and turned his hip towards the other, lowering his shoulder as the other's fist hammered at him, then Jeb's knee lifted. Garth's sudden movement caused the blow to land on his hip and not in the groin as had been intended. Even so, it knocked him temporarily off balance and he staggered heavily against the bar.

With a loud, bull-like roar of triumph, Jeb leapt in, his face alight with a savage exhilaration. It was this belief that the fight was virtually over, which proved to be the other's undoing. Garth feinted with his right hand, then stepped adroitly to one side, thrusting himself away from the bar with his leg, at the same time, swinging a short left to the man's body. It struck him in the soft part of the belly, just below the solar plexus. The other's mouth fell open, wide, air gushing out in a bleat of agony. For a long moment, he stood there, arms falling limply to his sides, body bent in the middle from the numbing force of the blow. His eyes were glazed and he swayed, scarcely aware of the yelling of his companions from the end of the bar.

His face was ashen, all of the blood having drained from it. Before he could recover, Garth drove another blow at his chin, felt it connect a little higher than he had intended, the cartilage of the other's nose squashing under his knuckles. He felt a sense of exhilaration pass through him as the other yelled hoarsely and staggered back, hands going up to his face.

Jeb growled a strong oath, rubbed the back of his hand across his battered face, stared for a moment at the blood smeared on his skin. The sight of his own blood enraged him, made him forget his pain. The crowd was shouting now, yelling encouragement to him. He squared his shoulders, moved in again, lips drawn back in a bestial snarl. Lowering his head to protect it from another blow, sawing in a big shuddering breath, he charged headlong at Garth. Garth was clear. He stood braced, waiting for the other. His head was clear now from that first hammer-fisted blow to the body. Not once looking away from the other, he waited. When Garth did not retreat before his flailing blows, Jeb tried a new tactic. Planting each foot solidly on the floor, he stood in the one spot, swinging with a more accurate style. Then Garth made his second mistake. Punching solidly and then dancing clear before the other could land any really damaging blows, he kept the other just sufficiently off balance to make it difficult for him to carry the fight forward as Jeb clearly wished to do. But now, Jeb anticipated him. Evidently he had learned his lesson from what had happened earlier in the fight. Thrusting his leg forward, he swung heavily from the waist, pivoting at the same time, feinting with his left, then swinging in a low right. The move took Garth completely by surprise. He had expected the other to bore in as he had been doing for the past few minutes, trusting to his superior weight to carry him forward. Throwing up his arm he tried to absorb the punishing impact of the blow, caught it on his upper arm. But the impact sent him staggering backward until he collided with one of the tables at his back. It gave under his weight, collapsing beneath him, sending him crashing to the floor. As he fell, Jeb leapt forward on top of him, crushing down with his weight.

Instinct made Garth bow his neck and twist to one side. In spite of this, all of the wind was knocked from his lungs and he felt the other's taloned fingers trying for his eyes, nails scratching across his face as he sought to gouge out his eyes from their sockets. He could feel the other's breath on his face, pantingly close.

Madly, he thrust up with his right knee, tried to heave the other from off him, but Jeb squirmed, wriggled to one side, then heaved himself up and loosened his fingers from Garth's face, clawing instead for his throat. Locking his fingers around the other's windpipe, he clamped a grip on his neck, squeezing with all of his strength. Garth felt his eyes bulge in their sockets. Inwardly, he knew that he had to break this murderous hold or it would mean the end. He could see the other's grinning face through a wavering red mist that floated in front of his vision.

Desperately, he struggled to draw air down into his aching, tortured lungs. For a moment, he hammered with his fists at the man's face, but the other merely twisted his lips into a sardonic smile and squeezed all the harder. The throbbing of blood in Garth's head was a dull thunder that threatened to drown out every other sound. Abruptly, he relaxed his body completely. For a split second, the move took Jeb by surprise. His hold around Garth's neck slackened slightly for the briefest fraction of a second, but it was long enough for Garth.

The edge of his right hand moved only six inches before it caught the other on the side of the head just below the ear. The bigger man gasped, fell over on his side. He tried helplessly to get to his feet, eyes bulging, his mouth widely open revealing his broken, stained teeth. Sucking air down into his chest, Garth pushed himself weakly to his feet, stood swaying for a moment, feeling the strength return gradually to his body. Unmindful of the man on the floor at his feet, he stood back, waiting for the other to rise, knowing that as soon as he did, he would hit him again and that this time, it would be the end.

For long moments, Jeb hung there, resting weakly on his hands and knees, his head hanging down limply between his arms, great sobbing gasps shuddering through his body. He seemed utterly spent, unable to move as Garth stood over him, waiting.

Then, abruptly, the other heaved himself forward, not on to his feet as Garth had expected, but forward along the floor, arms outstretched to their fullest extent, fingers clawing for the guns in the belt that lay near the bar. Swinging sharply, Garth saw the other's fingers close over the butt of one of the guns, jerked it free of the leather, twist it with his wrist, using the minimum of movement as he tried to roll over and bring the weapon to bear on Garth, intending to kill him from where he lay. It was out of the question for Garth to go for his own guns lying on the floor a few feet from where he stood. To try for them would mean instant death, for already the black hole in the end of the other's gun barrel was lining up on his chest, and Jeb's finger was tight on the trigger, the knuckle standing out white under the skin with the pressure he was exerting.

There was only one move to make to save his life, and Garth made it. His boot stamped down hard on the other's hand, pinning it to the floor. Jeb squirmed and threshed in agony as Garth increased the pressure, felt the bones in the man's wrist crack under his weight. The fingers loosened on the gun and a shrill bleat of agony burst from his lips. Bending, Garth picked up the gun from where it had fallen from the man's nerveless fingers, opened it and flipped out the shells from the chambers.

Then, watching the rest of the men at the bar out of the corner of his eye, he picked up his own belt and buckled it on. He ignored the injured man on the floor nearby, knowing that all of the fight had been knocked out of him. Turning to the watching bystanders, he said through tightly-clenched teeth: 'If there is anybody else who wants to make this fight a personal thing then I suggest that he steps outside into the street right now. He'll get an even chance, which is more than this hombre meant to give me.'

None of the men moved. He could see their tightening faces, but their gaze did not lock with his as he swept his scornful eyes over them. Picking up the glass from the bar, he downed the remainder of his drink in a swift gulp, tossed a coin on to the counter and walked towards the door. Reaching it, he paused, turned: 'I reckon I can't say much for the hospitality in this town. I've seen better in a dozen other trail towns along the frontier.' His glance fell to the man on the floor, striving to drag himself up into one of the chairs near the splintered table. 'Better get him to a doctor, have him take a look at that wrist of his.'

Thrusting open the doors, he stepped out into the street, felt the cool night air on his face, touched the bruises there where the other's fists had grazed the skin, and winced slightly. The street seemed to be empty, except for a small number of horses tethered to the hitchingrail outside the saloons along the street and the only sound was the hollow echoes of his own footsteps on the plankwalk and the raucous singing from the saloon further along the street.

He had almost drawn level with one of the narrow alleys that ran darkly off the main street to his right when he caught the sudden furtive movement in the dark shadows, whirled instinctively, right hand striking down for the gun at his waist. Then he halted the downward sweep abruptly as a soft voice said:

'Come over here, mister. I want to talk with you.'

Peering into the shadows, he saw the slender figure standing near the wall of the tall building. Even in the dimness, he recognized the woman who had been singing in the saloon, caught the faint odour of the perfume she wore. Her face was a pale blur in the darkness as he came up to her.

'What is it, Ma'am?' he asked quietly, wonderingly.

'I suppose that you know you've made enemies in there after what happened tonight,' she said softly.

'That comes as no surprise to me,' he told her. 'But why your interest in the matter?'

'Because I think I know why you're here.' She lifted her head and he knew that she was searching his face for something, maybe some sign that her ideas about him were right. 'They think that you're working with these outlaws in the hills. They're afraid. They're good men really, but when a thing like this happens, they're inclined to do things their own way and go off half-cocked, do things without stopping to think of the consequences. I know Jeb. Ordinarily, he'd never think of attacking a perfect stranger. He's been in fights before now, I'll admit that. But there's always been some reason for them and — '

'You don't have to apologize for them,' Garth said. 'But I have the feeling that you didn't come out here just to tell me this. You've got somethin' more on your mind.'

She was silent for a moment, then said quietly, her voice very soft. 'Someone in town sent for you, didn't they? They think that you might be able to stop these outlaws.'

'Maybe,' he said, his tone non-committal. 'But why do you think that?'

'You don't look the sort of man who would throw in his lot with outlaws, and yet you are a man who can handle a gun, and his fists as well. You've come up through a hard school and if you didn't fight against the law, then it seems to me you're fighting with it.'

'You're very observant,' he said. There was a faint note of admiration in his voice. 'I only hope that there are not too many in town who are as observant as you are.'

'Why do you say that? Surely if you let Sheriff Jessup know who you are and why you're here, he'll back you.'

'And once these outlaws discover that, it will make things a hundred times more difficult for me. Don't you see that I have to work under cover, without anyone knowing who I am? So long as the majority of the townsfolk, includin' the sheriff, think I may be in cahoots with these killers, it gives me a free hand. If they knew who I really am, then it would impose restrictions on me.'

'And you don't want that?' For a moment there was surprise and — he thought — bitterness in her voice. 'You'd rather run the risk of being killed, shot down from any shadow in town.'

'Never mind that,' he said to her. 'I know how to take care of myself.' He glanced around the corner of the alley, back in the direction of the saloon. A handful of men had stepped out, were standing on the boardwalk immediately outside the doors, so that the light fell full on them. One of them, held up by two others, was Jeb. His arm hung by his side and he was holding his wrist in his other hand, his features twisted into a grimace of anger and pain. He seemed to be arguing with the others, but in the end, they got their way and led him along the boardwalk back towards the centre of the town, evidently going along to the doctor's surgery to get the broken wrist attended to.

'Get back into the shadows,' Garth whispered urgently to the girl. One powerful arm swept out and pressed her back into the wall as he stood straight himself. The sound of the approaching men grew louder. Then they were moving past the mouth of the alley, less than ten feet away. None of them glanced round and a moment later, they had stepped up on to the boardwalk on the other side and disappeared from view.

Against Garth's rigid arm, he could feel the woman's heart beating rapidly. Very slowly, he took his arm away, drew up to his full height, glanced along the street after the men. They were still continuing along the boardwalk, still arguing in harsh tones. He let a deep breath sweep into his lungs and then out again.

'They've gone,' he said slowly.

She nodded. 'You'll have to keep watch every minute you're in town now,' she told him warningly. 'They won't stop until they've killed you and as far as Jeb is concerned, it may not be fair fight.'

'I'll be ready for them.' He licked his lips, rubbed the back of his hand over his check. His throat muscles still pained him where the other had squeezed them in his attempt to throttle him. He felt a stab of pain in his neck every time he swallowed. 'Is there anythin' you can tell me about this business? You must hear a lot in the saloon. Any little piece of information, no matter how trivial it seems right now. It might give me a clue.'

'Well, there was this man who rode in a little while before the stage was held up for the first time,' she said hesitantly.

'The man who called himself Smith. What about him?'

'Well, he said that he wanted to buy a plot of land and settle down here. He put up at the hotel, said he was going to stay for some time until he found a suitable place.'

'What's so strange about that?'

'Nothing really, I suppose. Except that he vanished on the same day that the stage was robbed. The clerk at the hotel says that he went out early that morning and never came back for his breakfast, or to collect his luggage. It's still in the hotel waiting for him, if he ever comes back to claim it.'

'I see.' Garth nodded his head slowly. That was a point that ought to have occurred to him after hearing what

Wayne Thorpe had had to say about this man named Smith. Obviously from what he was learning now, it had not been his real name, but in these frontier towns, a great many people lived under names which were not their own, and for a large variety of reasons. Maybe they were honestly trying to live down their past, maybe they were afraid of someone who might be following them, seeking vengeance. There could be several reasons why Smith had not given his real name. But the fact that he had left suddenly, had given no indication where he was going, and had left his luggage there, indicated one of two things to Garth. Either he had been killed that day and his body had never been discovered, or he was part of this outlaw gang and he had supplied them with the vital information they needed to hold up the stage carrying all that gold.

'There was another thing about him. He didn't look the sort of man who would settle down in a place like this.

He had that maverick look about him, and he'd been in a gunfight somewhere. He had this bandage around his head and he seemed to have something wrong with his left eye.'

'In what way?' asked Garth, suddenly interested.

'It was as if whatever had happened to his head, whether it was a bullet wound or not I don't know, had affected his sight. He had a strange way of looking at you, as if he couldn't see clearly out of that eye.'

'You're sure of this?' Garth caught her arm as he spoke, turning her to him.

'Quite sure.' She nodded her head emphatically. 'Does that help you?'

'I think you've told me all I need to know at the moment,' he said. He loosened his grip on her arm. 'But you'd better get back to the saloon before you're missed. If those outlaws do have anyone in town, keepin' an eye on things, they may notice that you've gone and start puttin' two and two together. And keep what you know about me quiet, won't you?'

'I want to see these men brought to justice as much as anyone else,' she said and for a moment there was a note of intense tightness in her voice so that he stared down at her in surprise, but he could see nothing on her face. A moment later, she turned on her heel and moved back into the alley. Then she was gone and there was only the faintest whiff of her perfume on the still air.

He paused there for a moment and then made his way slowly back to the hotel. There was a light burning in the doctor's surgery as he went by, and he guessed that Jeb was getting his wrist set. Smiling grimly to himself, he continued on, entered the lobby of the hotel, took his key from the clerk and started for the stairs. At the bottom he paused, turned and went back to the desk.

'Excuse me,' he said quietly. 'I understand that you had a Mr Smith registered here a month or so ago. He pulled out quite suddenly.'

The other's brows went up for a moment, then he swallowed his surprise, nodded his head. 'That's right, mister,' he affirmed. 'He left most of his luggage in his room. We still keep the room for him, just in case he does come back. He didn't pay for it for a period like this, but we have so few people staying here that I guess we can do that without any trouble. He may return and — well, he would then have to pay for the room during the past month, wouldn't he, and with business being so slack and all that. Well . . . '

'I understand.' Garth gave a faint smile. Everyone seemed to be after the last dollar they could lay their hands on. Still, it helped as far as he was concerned, so long as he did not arouse the other's suspicions too much.

'Which room did he have, do you know?'

The clerk glanced at the register on

the desk. 'Why, the room next to yours, Mr Martinue.'

'I see.' Garth gave a brief nod, climbed the creaking stairs and made his way along the corridor to his own room, unlocking the door, then stepping inside. Locking the door after him, he went over to the window and glanced out, not lighting the lamp, but feeling his way forward in the darkness. As he had hoped, there was a narrow veranda around the outside of the building and with a little luck, it would be possible for him to climb over on to the part outside the next window and get inside that room.

But that could wait until the morning. He had learned a lot during the first day here in Triple Peaks, far more than he had expected. The more he pondered over it, the more likely it seemed that the girl singer at the saloon had been right in her supposition that this stranger called Smith, who had occupied that room next to his, was one of the outlaw gang. He had, in all probability, joined the others on that morning when he had walked out of his hotel room, never to come back, and with the information he had gathered concerning the town and the apathy of the law, he had been able to build up the band into the strong, evil force it was at the present time.

But knowing this did not make it any easier to find these men, or to destroy them. He was, however, interested in what the girl had said about Smith having been wounded in the head and having difficulty in seeing out of his left eye. He recalled that the leader of the outlaws had been described as a man with a patch over his left eye. That seemed a little more than mere coincidence however one looked at it. More and more, the conviction grew that these two men were one and the same person.

If Smith had been hurt he would have gone to a doctor — not in Culver City, because unless he missed his guess, it would be a posse from there which would have been hunting him down when he had been hurt. No — he would have ridden for that small cowtown between Culver City and Triple Peaks, the one he had skirted on his way there, without actually riding through it. Whether the doctor there would talk or not, was something he did not know. But it was there, and possibly in Culver City, that he felt sure he would get more important information regarding this man he was seeking.

Closing the window against the chill of the night air, he pulled the heavy curtains over it, went back into the room and undressed in the darkness, hanging his gunbelt over the nearby chair. His bones and flesh felt bruised and weary after that fight with Jeb in the saloon. But in spite of this, he was asleep almost as soon as he closed his eyes.

When he woke, the grey dawn was just turning to the first scarlet flush which preceded the rising of the sun above the hills to the east. He ate his breakfast in the diner of the hotel, then made his way to Wayne Thorpe's office. The lawyer had arrived there a few minutes before he did, and welcomed him inside.

There was a quick look of surprise on the lawyer's face, quickly gone, as he glanced at Garth. 'You seem to have found trouble in town already,' he observed. 'What was it, some of the roughnecks looking for a fight?'

'Afraid so,' Garth nodded. 'But I did find out something that may help in trackin' down these outlaws. There seems little doubt that this Patch-Eye who leads the band and the man who called himself Smith and stayed here for a couple of days about a month ago are the same person.'

'And where does that get you?' inquired the other.

'I've learned that Smith had apparently been shot, or injured when he got here. He'd been wounded in the head and there was a bandage around it when he rode into town. I mean to ride out along the trail back to Culver City and ask a few questions of Sheriff Cantry there. I may also learn something from him about a message that Jessup sent last night from the telegraph office.'

'You realize, of course, that the trail back to Culver City will lead you through those hills where the outlaws have their hide-out?'

'I think I can get through them without too much trouble.'

'I hope so. They may be watching the trails out of town.'

'That's a possibility,' Garth conceded. 'But they can't watch every trail all of the time.'

For a moment, Thorpe's face was creased with worry. Then he shrugged. 'I guess you do know how to take care of yourself, at that,' he said quietly. 'This message you say Jessup sent last night. Do you know what it was?'

Garth nodded slowly. 'He sent it to Sheriff Cantry of Culver City. He wanted to know if I am a Texas Ranger.'

Thorpe let out a low whistle of surprise and consternation through his teeth. 'He's getting remarkably close to the truth, damn it,' he said harshly. 'This could make things very tricky for you, Garth.'

6

Outlaw!

In the tangled, impenetrable brush that grew along the higher slopes of the hills to the east of Triple Peaks, there were irregular, more open stretches of ground where mine workings, started and then abandoned before the Civil War, thrust deep holes into the solid rock. Now the home of those on the run from the law, away from the main trails through the hills, they provided a sanctuary for hundreds of the lawless breed.

From the small square window of the assay shack, Patch-Eye Turrell could look down the stony slope and see most of the deserted mine works that lay brooding in the harsh sunlight. A couple of rusted wagons, used for hauling the ore out of the mountain side, lay canted on their sides near the metal rails that vanished into the gaping hole torn out of the living rock. Just beyond them, he could make out the splintered wooden tops of the main shaft scaffoldings, now in a state of extreme decay.

It was a bleak enough outlook, even in the shimmering heat of the high noon sun, but it provided them with a place where they could hide out in safety between jobs. He had no certain knowledge how swiftly any attempt to capture them would be organised, nor how long it would be before the Rangers moved men into the territory in an attempt to break up the gang as they had once before. But he did know, that while they still held the initiative, they had to strike again. He had been thinking about the bank in Triple Peaks for a long while now, could draw on what he had learned during his brief stay there. It would be a relatively simple thing to knock over the bank. He had judged the sheriff there aright, he felt sure; a big man, but scared to his boots. A man who would not go up against a band of killers if he could possibly find a way out of it. He turned away from the window, glanced across at Kreb. The big man was seated at the small table, whittling away at a piece of wood with his knife. The blade glinted bluely in the shaft of sunlight that struck through the window.

Dufray and Tragge were lounging near the door, staring off into the bright sunlight.

'Patch-Eye,' said Dufray quietly.

Turrell did not glance directly at the other. He lit a cigarette and stared down at the smoke curling from the glowing tip.

'Patch-Eye,' said Dufray again. 'Why don't we just take what we've got now and head out of this goddamned territory? We're just askin' for trouble if we try anythin' more around these parts. The law ain't standin' still, you know. They'll be gettin' ready for us to move again and — '

Turrell's eyes remained on the cigarette and there was a kind of chill to his voice as he said thinly: 'I told you before, Dufray, to quit that sort of talk. There ain't nobody in the territory can stop us now.'

'But we can't go on like this for ever.'

'Why not? So long as we got them on the run, we can take any bank or stage we like.'

'Sure. But all the time we got to stay here like hunted animals. We've got more'n fifty thousand dollars stashed away. What's the good of it if we can't spend any of it'?'

'We stay here because I say so,' Turrell snapped, some of the steel showing through in his tone. 'Besides, I've got plans for taking the bank in Triple Peaks and soon.'

'That's askin' for trouble,' put in Tragge harshly. He levered his body away from the wooden upright of the door. 'That's where they'll be waitin' for us.'

'No — that's the last place they'll

expect us to attack. Jessup's nothin' more than a scared rabbit. He won't try anythin'. Besides, I want to know what's been happenin' there while we've been up here in the hills. I've got ideas of bringin' in more men.'

Dufray calmed himself with an effort; there was no point in getting excited. 'Where do you figure on gettin' these men, Turrell?'

'From the Bar X ranch. Ain't you forgettin' that they're all set against the town? I aim to build this band up into the biggest thing this territory has ever seen.'

'When?'

'When I'm good and ready.'

'And all the time, we're forced to hide out here, living in this god-forsaken place. That money's no good to us where it is, hidden away inside that mine shaft.'

Turrell looked up now, faintly grinning. 'Dufray, if I didn't know you better, I'd say you was gettin' scared.'

'I'm simply facin' the facts.'

'They don't mean a goddamned thing,' retorted the other harshly. He went over to the doorway. His glance went down the slope. 'The only fact I'm facin' is that there'll be several thousand in gold and dollar bills in that bank now and I aim to get it. Now get your horses and be ready to ride. If we start out now, we should be close to Triple Peaks by nightfall.'

'You figurin' on ridin' into town tonight?' Kreb eased his big frame out of the chair at the table, stretched himself, and tried to keep the surprise out of his voice.

'It'll be the last place they'll be lookin' for us,' said Turrell quietly. 'There are some empty shacks on the northern end where we can hole up for the night.'

Kreb thought that over for a moment, then boomed out a loud laugh. 'I like the idea, Turrell,' he said harshly. 'We squat right under their noses for the night and then take the bank in the mornin'.'

In the directly above them light of noon, they rode down the ever narrowing canyon from the mine, into the thick scrub that grew out of the arid, rocky ground at the bottom of the slope which angled down the lee of the tall hill. It seemed incredible that anything could grow in this terrible wilderness, Turrell reflected as he sat hunched forward in the saddle, head lowered against the hot wind which blew down from the mountain crests high above them, lifting occasional flurries of dust and hurling it against them. But somehow, this tough wiry grass and the stunted bushes managed to suck enough moisture from the thin, dry soil to exist.

The three men were strung out close behind him as they entered a rocky defile, only wide enough for one man at a time to ride through and even then his legs scraped the rock on either side. The glare of the sun was a sickening thing and at times, he heard Dufray cursing loudly and harshly behind him. Once, he half turned his head to snap at the other as he felt his nerves scraped raw by the heat and glare, then stopped himself, biting down the angry words. It would solve nothing and they had plenty ahead of them without fighting among themselves. But Dufray would have to be watched. It wouldn't do to have him backing out on them at the wrong moment.

He led them along the defile, then across an open bench of ground and into a slope that led them eventually into timber. At the bottom, there was a wide stream that splashed over a stony bed and they watered their mounts here, pausing to let them blow.

Squatting on his heels on the edge of the stream, Kreb said: 'I've been thinking, Turrell.'

'What about?' asked the other, leaning his back against the trunk of a tree.

'About where the three of us were

before you showed up. We'd been runnin' from the law for months and when you rode into our camp that evenin' we were just figurin' on ridin' out of this territory and headin' south to Texas. Now we've got more money than we can ever spend, even if we lit out for New Mexico right now.'

'And this is nothin' to what we can have in a few months' time,' Turrell affirmed. 'I've got plans that could make us richer than you've ever dreamed.'

'And you think we can go on like this without the law decidin' to take a hand in the game?' queried Dufray.

'By the time the law decides to take a hand we'll be ready for 'em,' declared Turrell confidently. 'In the meantime, leave the worryin' to me. All you have to do is obey orders. Understand?'

For a moment, Dufray glared at him, then he let his gaze slide away, nodded slowly. 'All right, Turrell, but don't say I didn't give you warnin' if anythin' goes wrong.'

Turrell tightened his lips, looked around at the other two men. 'Either of you feel like this?' he asked. 'I reckon we'd better get things straightened out right now, before we go any further.'

Kreb shrugged his massive shoulders. 'You're in charge, Turrell,' he said thickly. 'I ain't had any complaints so far about the way you've handled things. Guess we can go on like this as far as I'm concerned.'

Tragge nodded in agreement.

'Good. Then saddle up. We've still got some distance to cover before dark.'

With Turrell leading, they splashed across the stream, followed the narrow, half-seen trail through the underbrush on the other side, their horses going slower now because of the nature of the terrain. Gradually, the slope became steeper, they were forced to wind their way up switchback courses where, in long ages past, some geological upheaval had twisted this rock into weird shapes and channels.

At the rim of the long ridge, the pines grew less and they paused for a moment to look back. They could just make out the stream, far below them, glinting between the trees. There was no movement down there, not that they had expected any; but as they were making their way down a loose shale slide, half an hour later, they spotted a rider in the far distance, cutting through one of the wide stage trails that led through the hills.

Kreb pointed him out, said harshly: 'Somebody spurrin' his mount fast, Turrell. Looks as though he's ridden out from Triple Peaks.'

Turrell narrowed his eyes against the pouring sunglare, tried to make out the rider, but the distance was too great and the dust cloud thrown up by the horse hung about him as he rode, obscuring him for long intervals of time. At last, he shrugged.

'Reckon he's nobody of importance,' he said through tight lips. 'Can't do anythin' against us anyway and it's unlikely he's carryin' anythin' valuable with him.'

They set their mounts to the westward trail that wound snake-like down the face of the ridge. Ahead of them, some miles away, there was open country dipping and rolling in long gradual swells right out to the far horizon. But until they reached the prairie, they were forced to ride slow, keeping a tight rein on their mounts. There were tricky patches of ground to cross, long wrinkles in the earth formed when the hills had been made and they rode their mounts down them, straight-legged, sitting forward in the saddles to enable the horses to keep their balance. Halfway through the afternoon, they were riding through the gigantic rock formations that formed the lower foothills of the range. Great boulders that lay in tumbled confusion on the wild brush of narrow valley floors. The rocks slowed them down more than Turrell had anticipated. He had been confident of reaching Triple Peaks before nightfall but the sun was sinking swiftly towards the hills in the far west while they were making their way down to the rolling prairie, with still the best part of ten miles to go.

Daylight was beginning to fade from the stretching arch of the heavens once they reached the flatter, more open, country, but here they could give their horses their heads and they rode hard in a long, wide sweep that took them well away from the main trails.

The dark, shadowy shape of Triple Peaks, rising up from the dimness, was sighted just as the sun vanished behind the hills in a violent, soundless explosion of scarlet and crimson light. For several moments, the western sky was a blaze of flame. Then the redness faded, the greens and blues came surging in from the east to swamp out the last traces of sunset and the heat began to diminish as a cooler breeze sprang up, robbing the air of its oven-like heat.

It was a blue world now, abrim with the smell of the hills. The dusk lingered for a little while, then gave way, reluctantly almost it seemed, to the night and the first of the sky soldiers appeared in the east.

Turrell eased himself in his saddle, making it as easy as possible for his mount. He had long since learned that for a man to be able to ride long distances, he had to give first consideration to his horse. Beside him, hard-faced, rode the rest of the men.

An hour later, they came upon the town from the north, cutting in along a narrow, seldom-used trail. Turrell halted his mount when they were still half a mile from the town, signalled to the others to do likewise. They clustered around him in a tight knot.

'Even better than I figured,' Turrell said in a low voice. He rolled a smoke, lit it with his hands cupped around his face, head lowered so that the brief orange flare of the match would not be seen from a distance. He blew the smoke out in front of him, holding the reins slackly in his hand. 'There's an old warehouse on this side of town. Nobody ever uses it now. At first light, we'll get into position. We don't want to ride towards the bank in a bunch. That would arouse too much suspicion. This is how we're goin' to do it. Better listen carefully because I don't want any mistakes tomorrow.'

Quietly, he explained the plan to them, saw Kreb nod his head in agreement several times. There were no questions when he had finished. The plan was very similar to what they had used before when robbing one of the banks in the territory.

After Turrell had smoked his cigarette, they gigged their mounts forward, walking them now. They made steady progress with only the faint sound of hooves in the dust accompanying them, until as near as Turrell could determine, they were almost in the outskirts of the town. Here, he ordered the others to dismount and lead the horses in. Moving more slowly, feeling their way through the darkness here, unlit by any gleam of light, they came to a very narrow spacing between two tall buildings and squeezed their way through. In the pale starshine, it was just possible to make out the contours and angles of the buildings that loomed up on either side of them. In the distance, there was the sound of raucous singing from the saloons, an occasional gunshot that disturbed the stillness, but that was all. Apart from this, the town seemed unnaturally quiet.

As he walked forward, Turrell peered into the shadows on either side of him, seeking some familiar landmark, trying to recall his last visit here, when he had filed away this information against the time, such as this, when it would be needed. A few moments later, he was confident that he knew exactly where he was. Pausing in front of a long, low building, he nodded towards it.

'In here!' he said quietly. 'And no noise.'

One by one, they led their mounts inside. The place had been a storehouse for a variety of goods, including straw and hay and in one corner, they found some which did not seem to have deteriorated and gave the horses a feed.

Once they were settled down, he went over to the opening in the wall that served as a window, peered out into the darkness. Now he waited, leaning on his left side, feeling the cool rush of air against his face and neck. He looked at the black shadow of the street below him and he thought: It looks like a great black rug, waiting to be rolled up.

Turning back to the others, he said curtly: 'Better get some sleep. We'll have plenty to do in the mornin'.'

Stretching himself out on the hard floor, with only the curve of the saddle for a pillow, he closed his eyes and was asleep in a moment. He woke once or twice during the night, thinking he heard something in the street outside, but whenever he forced himself to concentrate his senses on it, there was nothing. Cats roaming the darkness possibly, he thought, then drifted back into sleep again.

In the pale grey light of an early dawn, they ate the cold jerked beef they had brought with them, washed it down with cold water from their canteens. The horses remained out of sight but there was no one in the narrow alley in front of the building on any of the occasions whenever Turrell glanced out.

Ten o'clock, and they saddled the horses inside the warehouse. Around them, the town had been awake for some hours and there was the occasional beat of horses' hooves along the main street somewhere in the near distance. Smoking, Turrell leaned his weight against the upright near the open window, waited while the others tightened the cinches under their mounts' bellies. He felt the smoke lacing painfully across his good eye, but ignored it. Patch-Eye Turrell. He had lasted for more than fifteen years, first down near the Texas border and now up here, more than a thousand miles from where he had first started. Down there, he had been something of a legend. Soon, if he had his way, it would be the same here, and this time, he would not make the same mistakes as he had then, mistakes which had eventually, inevitably, brought about his downfall and the deaths of the men who had ridden with him. The flesh on his face was drawn down tight into his bones, making him look twenty years older than he really was, and his good eye, glaring out at the world, held a terrible expression.

Standing there, he went over the details of the coming raid on the bank in his mind. There had been a time when he had looked forward to such a task with a feeling of trepidation, almost amounting to one of a premonition of disaster. Now, things were different. With success, had come a different outlook on things. He knew that everything had been taken care of, that the chances were all loaded in their favour. The townfolk of Triple Peaks would be thinking that he and his men were holed up somewhere in the hills fifteen miles or so to the east. They would not be expecting them here in town, would not dream that they had been sleeping under their very noses during the night. He smiled grimly to himself. Everything went according to instinct now, he told himself, crushing out the butt of the cigarette on the dusty floor as he saw that the others had finished getting their mounts ready. He went forward into danger like a lobo wolf, scenting it, and actually looking forward to meeting it halfway.

Five minutes later, Kreb rode out into the narrow alley, moved away from the middle of town, vanished around the corner of one of the tall buildings. Cutting through the tangled web of alleys that formed a maze in this part of town, he moved around by a circuitous route to the main street, his hat pulled well down over his eyes, then rode slowly along the dusty main street, reaching the saloon close by the bank, and hitched his horse to the rail, striding purposefully over to the board-walk and sinking down on to his haunches on the edge of it, legs thrust out in front of him, smoking a cigarette, head bowed forward on his chest, like a man who was half-sleeping there in the growing heat of the day.

Dufray and Tragge rode in from the other direction, cut out of one of the side streets into the square in the middle of town, left their mounts close by and went over to the wooden bench around the bole of the huge cotton-wood, where they seated themselves unobtrusively, apparently taking very little interest in anything that went on around them.

They were there for ten minutes before Turrell finally appeared near the end of the main street. He walked his horse forward with a deceptive slow-ness, reined up almost in front of the bank, sat tall in the saddle for a long moment, turning his head to look about him. It was an all-embracing stare, but for the most part it was directed towards the three men, waiting and watchful in the street. While he sat there, a couple of customers went into the bank, and there was a wait until one of them came out, thrust his wallet into the inside pocket of his long coat and walked over to one of the stores, going inside and closing the door behind him.

Moving slowly, Turrell got down from the saddle, moved towards the hitching post and tied his mount to the rail. It was the signal for the others to move. Unobtrusively, they converged on the bank. To a casual glance, it appeared as though they were completely discon- nected entities, moving along paths of their own, having nothing in common. Kreb dropped his half-smoked cigarette into the dirt in front of the bank, ground it into the dust with his heel, paused for a moment, scratching the back of his head as though perplexed at something.

While this had been going on, Turrell had walked into the bank with Dufray

211

and Tragge close on his heels. Once inside the building, they split up. Tragge stayed close to the door, while Dufray went across to the window and leaned his back and shoulders against the wall, surveying the scene through narrowed eyes. His thumbs were stuck into his gunbelt and he appeared an innocent bystander, having no interest at all in what was happening there.

Near the teller's cage, Turrell stopped, thrust a cigarette between his lips and made to strike a match. His head was lowered as he did so, his one eye taking in all that was happening; the two tellers behind the wire, a woman standing near the other counter and the customer they had seen go in, but not come out, moving slowly away from the cage.

Lowering his hands, Turrell jerked the twin Colts from their holsters and fanned them out. In a loud voice that carried to every corner of the bank, he said 'All right, everybody. This is a hold-up. All of you — flat on the floor with your arms out in front of you and nobody gets hurt.'

The woman screamed thinly, a faint sound, then slid in a faint to the floor in front of the teller's cage. Turrell knew that he would not have to watch her any further. The customer obeyed with alacrity, dropping flat on to his face, arms in front of him. The guns in the hands of the other two outlaws rapidly convinced the tellers that resistance was useless. Turrell moved forward to one of the cages, thrust the barrel of the Colt between the bars and said thinly: 'Don't try anythin', I don't want to have to kill you, but if you don't do exactly as I say, you're dead. Understand?'

'Yes.' The teller nodded quickly, his adam's apple bobbing up and down in his scrawny throat. He backed away from the cage, then moved forward as Turrell ordered: 'Now open up this thing.'

The other hesitated, threw a quick glance over his shoulder, then flicked his gaze back to Turrell, but not quick enough. Out of the corner of his eye, Turrell saw the man near the back of the bank, close to the vaults, a man who had a shotgun cradled in his arms, who was, at that moment, levelling it on him, his finger tight on the trigger. The Colt in Turrell's fist blasted, the sound oddly loud in the confining space of the bank. The slug took the man full in the chest, hurled him back against the front of the vault, arms outspread, his body hanging there as if in a state of crucifixion, the gun dropping from lifeless fingers, to crash on to the floor. For several incredible seconds, the other remained in that position. Then his legs gave and he slid slowly down on to the floor, his whole body utterly limp and lifeless.

'Come on,' Turrell snarled at the teller, who stood stricken, his face numbed with shock. 'Open up and hurry!'

With shaking fingers, the other hurried to obey. Unlocking the mesh cage, he moved back, arms lifted high over his head, features ashen and bloodless, as the outlaw leader vaulted the gate and dropped lightly down on the other side. Scooping up the handful of bills on the counter, he thrust them into the bag he carried, then motioned to the vaults. 'All right. Through there and bring out what gold you have.' He pushed the other in front of him, twisting his arm savagely behind his back to urge him forward. Stumbling, the other moved towards the vaults, opened them up, pausing instinctively to stare down at the twisted body of the dead man on the floor, the front of his shirt stained with a widening patch of red.

'Put it all in there,' Turrell said, holding out the wheat sack. He did not turn his head to make sure that everything was under control in the bank itself, leaving that up to Dufray and Tragge. Outside, Kreb would be watching the horses, and be ready for any trouble. Once that shot was heard, there might be some citizens who would come running to see what was wrong. He knew he could rely on Kreb to hold them off until they all got clear.

The teller filled the wheat sack with the bars of gold, shaking like a leaf as he did so, occasionally throwing fearful glances in the direction of the dead man.

Grimly, Turrell told him: 'Just keep on shovelling that gold in there and hurry, and you won't go the same way as he did. If he'd done as he was told, he'd still be alive now. Don't do to be a hero at a time like this. Especially when it ain't your money we're taking.'

The other said nothing, but continued to haul the gold blocks out of the vaults until the sack was full. Turrell took it, moved back to the teller's cage, handed it over to Tragge, then took the empty one which the other had brought with him. When this was full, the vaults were empty.

'Now get down on the floor like the others and don't try to do anythin' funny,' Turrell ordered harshly. 'If you put you head up within the next five minutes, you'll get it blown off by one of my men standing by the door. You understand that?'

The teller nodded his head quickly, stretched himself out on the floor, arms and legs out-thrust. Turrell watched him for a moment, then climbed back over the counter, moved away towards the door.

'Hurry!' said Dufray. 'There's trouble outside. Somebody must've heard that shot. What the hell happened back there?'

'Somebody tried to be a hero,' Turrell said grimly. He turned to look over the prone bodies of the customers and the tellers, then jerked the barrel of his gun in the direction of the street. 'Let's get movin'. If we hang around here any longer, there may be a reception committee waitin' for us along the street. You know what to do if there is.'

The two men nodded, raced for the door. Carrying the heavy wheat sack, filled almost to the brim with the gold blocks, Turrell moved after them. In the doorway, he paused, glanced back. Everyone hugged the floor closely, obviously not wanting to take any chances, possibly knowing that one man had tried it and now he was lying dead with part of his chest ripped away by a heavy slug.

There came a scattered volley of gunshots as they raced out on to the boardwalk. Kreb had the horses ready, was waiting for them, occasionally throwing shots towards the far corner of the square. Turrell peered through the strong sunglare, made out the figures of the men crouched down behind a couple of rain barrels and the horse trough. Bringing up his gun, he loosed off a couple of shots, saw some wood fly in chips where the bullets struck. There was a vivid orange blast of flame from the shadows and at his back, the window of the bank went in with a resounding crash as the buckshot struck it. Glass shards fell into the dust beside him as he moved for his horse, tied the wheat sack behind the saddle and swung himself up. A slug whined through the air close to his head with a vicious hum of metal cutting wind and he ducked instinctively in the saddle, head low over his horse's neck. Kicking spurs into the animal's flanks, he drove it forward along the street, the other men thundering along at his back.

Switching his gaze from side to side, he saw the door of the sheriff's office jerk open, saw the big shape of Sheriff Jessup step out on to the boardwalk and then jerk back in again, caught the sungleam of blued metal in the lawman's hand a second before Jessup fired. There was a loud yell from immediately behind him and he knew that one of the others had been hit, but how bad he did not know. There was no time now to stop and find out. If whoever it was couldn't keep in the saddle and stay up with them, then it was just too bad. It would mean one less to share the gold when they got to the hills.

More revolvers were firing on both sides of them as they raced their mounts along the length of the main street. The shotgun from behind them roared again, but the slugs went wild, although from along the boardwalk, other men began shooting methodically at them as they raced out of town.

As his horse came abreast of a group of men crouched behind the window of a grocery store, Turrell swung slightly in the saddle, holding the Colt in his left hand. He sent several shots in through the glass, heard it crash under the impact. The firing from inside the store lessened and then stopped altogether as he rode on. Leaning forward in his saddle, he led the others out of Triple Peaks.

Once they were clear, giving their horses their head, riding hell for leather to put as much distance between themselves and the town as possible, before Jessup got a posse collected and came after them, Turrell had time to think. The fury of the opposition had been greater than he had anticipated. It must have been that shot when he had been forced to kill the bank employee at the vault that had given them away and given the townsfolk sufficient time in which to organise themselves in spite of all the efforts that Kreb had made to scatter them.

'Slow down, Turrell,' called Tragge from behind him. 'I've been hit. I can't keep up at this pace.'

Cursing under his breath, Turrell jerked hard on the reins. Tragge was slumped forward in the saddle, his face white, lips pushed tightly together in a grimace of pain.

'Where are you hit?' he asked harshly, moving his horse over to the other.

'In the shoulder.' Tragge bit the words out through tightly-clenched teeth. He forced himself to sit straight in the saddle. There was a patch of blood on his shirt and, reaching forward, Turrell tore it across with his strong fingers, glanced at the wound. It was evident that the slug was still in the flesh, probably lodged against the shoulder blade. But there was nothing they could do there and the longer they delayed here, the more they increased the chances of being captured by the posse which must surely be getting formed back in town. Whatever Jessup might feel about things, he could not stand by and do nothing, now that the outlaws had hit the bank there. He had been elected to the post of sheriff and he would have to form a posse and follow their trail, however reluctant he might be to do it.

'We'll have to get back into the hills before we can take a look at that wound,' Turrell said sharply, his tone hard and devoid of any feeling. 'Think you can make it there? Once we get under cover, I'll take that piece of lead out. But we can't stop here.'

Tragge swallowed thickly, then nodded his head with an effort. 'I'll make it,' he said tautly. 'Ain't nobody goin' to get my share of that money.'

It was almost as if he had divined their thoughts.

'Then let's get movin',' Turrell snapped, as if he had not heard what the other had said. 'That damned posse will be on our trail any minute now. And they'll have too many men ridin' with them for us to take on, especially with a wounded man.'

With Tragge clinging precariously to the saddle, they rode at full speed along the dusty trail, heading east, away from Triple Peaks, towards the tall range of mountains that loomed high in front of them across the smooth prairie. They were long, drawn-out hours during the rest of the morning and afternoon. No clouds touched the blue-white mirror of the heavens and the sunglare beat down on them with an almost physical pressure, like the smack of a mighty hand against the ground and anyone who dared to travel on it during the time of the full, blazing heat. Sickened by the glare that was reflected at them from the burnt ground, nauseated by the bitter smell of the sage, they at last came to the narrow stream over which they had ridden the previous day on their way into Triple Peaks.

Climbing the steep trail, they made their way slowly to the top, the sweat soaking into their shirts so that they chafed their bodies with every move-ment they made. Angrily, Turrell wiped the back of his hand over his forehead, then reined up his mount and turned, staring back along they way they had come, shading his eyes against the sun. Far off, in the distance, he made out the tiny cloud of white dust, no bigger than a man's hand. It marked the position of the hard-riding posse which had been on their trail since they had pulled out of Triple Peaks. He smiled grimly to himself. They would never find them now. Here in the hills, there were too many trails, too many smooth, stony patches where their horses left no prints, where not even a coyotero could track them.

'What do you think, Patch-Eye?'

asked Kreb. He inclined his head towards the bunch of riders.

'Forget 'em,' Turrell said quietly, with conviction. 'They'll never find us in here and I reckon they know it. They may try to search a little ways into the brush and then they'll head back to town, their conscience satisfied. They did their best and it wasn't their fault they didn't catch up with us in time, before we'd slipped into the hills.' He uttered a sharp bark of a laugh, motioned to Tragge, leaning limply in the saddle. 'Reckon you can manage it the rest of the way, Tragge?'

The other's voice was weak as he muttered: 'I think so. But don't waste time. This shoulder hurts like hell. It's as if there's a red hot poker being twisted in the flesh.'

'We'll get that lead out of you as soon as we get back to camp,' Turrell affirmed. 'In the meantime, just stick there in the saddle. Not much further to go now.'

He led the way down into the thickly

tangled brush, through the stunted bushes and trees that grew in a wild profusion here. In places, the trail was virtually nonexistent, yet Turrell rode forward without hesitation, always cutting up to the higher ledges and ridges that loomed over them in the late afternoon light. He did not bother to look back and check on the posse on their trail, but was content to ride ahead, secure in the knowledge that they had nothing to fear from those men.

The shadows were long over the gorges and rugged rocks by the time they entered the canyon leading up to the old mine workings. Past the big wooden cyanide vats used for extracting the gold and silver from the ore, they tethered their mounts near the shack and went inside. By now, Tragge could scarcely stand. He had lost a lot of blood during the day-long ride out from town and he made no move to resist as Turrell got him into a chair and stripped the blood-stained shirt from his body, tossing it on to the floor.

'Kreb. Start a fire and get me some boiling water. I'll try to get this slug out of him and patch him up.'

'He looks in a bad way now,' said Dufray harshly. He stood staring down at Tragge, sprawled in the chair. 'You sure you know what you're doin'?'

'I've had to doctor more men with gunshot wounds and carryin' slugs inside them than you've ever dreamed of,' he said with a faint note of contempt in his voice. Ignoring the other, he cleaned the wound with cold water, waited while Kreb had the fire started. Then he took out the long-bladed bowie knife and placed it in the flames.

Tragge opened his eyes at this, stared down at the knife for a moment and a visible shudder ran through his frame. For a second, he struggled to get to his feet, but he was so weak that he couldn't make it and flopped down in the chair again, his head lolling to one side. He was scarcely conscious.

Kreb said tightly: 'He looks as if he's passed out, Patch-Eye.'

Turrell gave a brief nod. 'Maybe that's best,' he said. 'He won't feel too much that way.'

Without proper doctor's instruments and with only the learning he had picked up the hard way along the trail, he knew that there was always a good chance that Tragge would not live, even if he managed to get the piece of lead out of his shoulder. It was a nasty wound. The slug had hit him obliquely, tearing in through the flesh, before embedding itself close to the shoulder bone. Whether or not it had actually chipped and splintered the bone he could not tell as yet. If it had, then it was going to be even more difficult to get the slug out and patch the other up.

'Get me the knife,' he said sharply. Kreb went over to the fire and withdrew the knife, bringing it over to him. Turrell waited for the blade to cool, wiped away a little blood which still oozed from the gaping wound, and probed with the knife tip into the torn and mangled flesh.

Even in the depths of his unconsciousness, Tragge moaned deep within his throat and a further shudder went through his body. His teeth sank into his lower lip, and there were flecks of blood on it as Turrell probed further.

'You'd better hold him down,' he said, motioning to Kreb. The black-bearded giant came forward, stood with his huge hands grasping Tragge's shoulders, pinning him motionless to the chair. It was doubtful if the other could have moved even if he had been conscious.

'That's better.' Turrell went on with his task. The wound began to bleed again, making it more difficult to see what he was doing. More than once, he was inclined to stop it, to bind up the other's shoulder with strips of cloth torn from his shirt and patch him up as best he could that way. There had been men he had heard of who had lived for years with a piece of lead inside them.

But he put the thought out of his head whenever it came into his mind. He had started and it was up to him to finish it.

Again, the other moaned, would have twisted in the chair had it not been for Kreb's hands holding him immobile. At length, Turrell felt the tip of the knife blade touch something hard, yet yielding. He bent forward a little, continued to probe, easing the object out of the wound. It came slowly out, a dulled piece of metal, just recognizable as a bullet.

'There,' he said tightly. 'Now we can patch him up.' He knew that there was sweat on his forehead, but did not wipe it off. 'Soak me some strips of cloth from his shirt in that boiling water,' he ordered, without lifting his head. 'I can do no more for him now. The rest is up to his own constitution.'

He finished binding up the other's shoulder, then straightened his back. 'That ought to do it,' he muttered. 'Now let's check that gold.'

Tragge slept uneasily most of that

night, but by morning, when he wakened, he was conscious and clear-minded. His shoulder was stiff and ached with a numb agony. As Turrell came into the assay shack, he asked: 'Did we manage to throw off that posse?'

Turrell nodded briefly. 'They must've followed up to the edge of the brush and then decided to go back. Relax, they'll never find us here. We've outwitted them once and we can do it again.'

'What do you mean by that?' asked Kreb, standing in the doorway.

Turrell grinned viciously. 'One more big haul like yesterday's and we'll be set for life. We can split what we have and head south for the border. A life of ease and luxury for all of us.'

'Why not go right now?' put in Dufray tersely. 'The whole territory is sure to be hummin' like a hornet's nest by now. They won't sit around and wait for us to strike at some other bank. They'll be settin' up traps all over the place, for us to ride into. I've heard of it happenin' that way before. Don't see why it should be any different for us. That Jessup ain't no fool, whatever else you might think he is.'

'Mebbe not,' Turrell agreed. 'But we'll lay low for a little while and then, when the time is right, we'll hit the last place on earth they'll expect us to attack.'

Kreb raised his brows a little. 'Where's that?' he asked tautly.

Turrell's grin broadened. 'The bank at Triple Peaks — where else?' he said challengingly.

7

The Wild Breed

Garth Martinue rode into Culver City shortly before ten o'clock in the evening on the second day after leaving Triple Peaks. He tied his mount in front of the sheriff's office and started for the steps, but at the walk, he glanced out of the corner of his eye and noticed the lawman heading towards him from the far side of the street.

'Saw you ride into town,' said Cantry. 'Figured you might be along sooner or later. Come on into the office and rest yourself. It must've been a long, hard ride across that desert.'

'It was,' Garth agreed. It felt good to sit down in the high-backed chair in the lawman's office and stretch his legs out in front of him. The other brought a glass of whiskey, set it in his hand, poured one for himself, then sank down into the chair at the back of the long, score-marked desk, and placed his feet on top of it, tipping his hat on to the back of his head.

'I got a message from Jessup in Triple Peaks askin' about you.' The other took out the sheet of paper from the drawer in his desk, spread it flat in front of him. 'He seems mighty suspicious of you. Any reason why?'

'I figure he's suspicious of everybody who rides into town these days. That outlaw band that's operatin' from there is givin' him a mite of trouble. But I guess it's mainly because he doesn't like the job he's been landed with now that there's some real trouble broken out there.'

'I can guess his feelings,' acknowledged the other. 'From what I've heard this is some mean outfit. We've been hit ourselves once. They got away with plenty, I can tell you. They're cunning and smart. They know just how to go about it and they hit us before we were aware of it.'

'That's why I'm here. I got a lead on the leader of this gang from the singer in one of the saloons. Seems this *hombre* rode into town, saying his name was Smith, booked in at the hotel, then pulled out without warning on the very mornin' that the stage was held up for the first time. From what I found out, he had been hurt pretty bad by a bullet that must've creased his skull. He'd had it bandaged up and I found out that it was the doctor in that cowtown along the trail who tended him.'

'You sure it was the same man?' Interest sparked the other's tone.

'No doubt about it. That crease in his skull had affected his left eye. The doctor finally admitted that the chances were this *hombre* wouldn't be able to use it after a little while. Something about damage to a nerve. But it fits this outlaw who leads this gang. He wears a patch over his left eye.'

Cantry nodded his head slowly. Surprise showed momentarily on his face. 'We had a brush with an outlaw, a killer named Turrell. He was headed up from Texas with half a dozen posses ridin' his trail. We lost him in the desert, but I'm sure one of my men hit him on the side of the skull, nearly knocked him out of the saddle. If he kept on ridin' the same way, he'd end up in Triple Peaks.'

'How long ago was this?'

Cantry pursed his lips, stared down at the whiskey bottle, 'About a month, maybe a mite longer.'

'So it could be the same man,' mused Garth. 'I've heard of this *hombre* Turrell. His gang was smashed a while back down near the Texas border. He was the only one to get away.'

'That's right.' Cantry opened another drawer in his desk, rifled through the papers there, then pulled out a faded wanted poster, slid it across the desk to Garth. 'That's him. He may be changed a little by now. That eye patch will make a difference, although it's bound to be distinctive.'

Garth studied the man's face intently. It was a cruel face, with no spark of humanity showing in any line of it; the sort of face he would have expected an outlaw killer like this to have. After he had perused the picture for a few moments, he slid it back to Cantry.

'Sooner or later this killer is goin' to make a mistake and I intend to be around when he does,' he said ominously.

'He's a dangerous man,' warned the other, sliding the picture back with the others inside the desk. 'He must be to have led that outlaw gang down near the border for so long and still get away when the Rangers closed in on him.'

Garth nodded musingly. He bit the end off a cigar, lit it and blew out the smoke through narrowly parted lips. 'And what are you goin' to do about the message that Jessup sent?'

Cantry grinned faintly, stared down

at the paper in front of him. 'I'm not sure what to do. I guessed you might be ridin' into town and I held off sending any answer until you did.'

'I'd be obliged if you merely said that you knew nothin' about me at all for the present,' Garth said, after a brief pause. 'The less Jessup knows, the better.'

'You think he may be workin' with these outlaws?'

'No — I'm sure he isn't. But he's scared, deep down inside. If he could see a way of throwing up this job, he'd do it like a shot now that he knows what it can really mean, that there's a chance of him gettin' killed in the furtherance of his duties as sheriff.'

'I'll send that message off tonight,' nodded the other. Fishing for a pencil, he wrote it out, got to his feet and walked to the street door, calling to somebody in the shadows. Out of the corner of his eye, Garth saw the oldster who came out of the darkness, took the note which Cantry handed to him and then vanished again into the night. The sheriff came back and seated himself in the chair once more, relaxing. 'Jessup will get that sometime tonight,' he said, grinning. 'In the meantime, what are your plans?'

'I'll stay here overnight, then pull out in the morning. I'd like any information at all you can give me on Turrell or any of the other lawless breed who you know to be hidin' out in this part of the territory, particularly in those hills.'

'You figure that Turrell got the men to follow him from that bunch?'

'It makes sense, doesn't it?'

'I suppose you could be right.' Cantry poured a second drink for them, tossed his own down in a single gulp as if he needed it. 'Those hills are several miles long and over a mile wide, full of old Indian trails and abandoned mine workings, left there since before the War. Even if you had a half dozen posses, you wouldn't find them in there in a year. They know every inch of those trails and you could ride within a couple of feet of them without even knowin' they were there.'

'That's the way I had it figured. That's why I reckon the only way we'll ever force a showdown with them is to lay a trap of our own. Get them to ride into Triple Peaks and seal off every exit. That way, we can finish them.'

'Could be that this has no bearin' on the problem,' said the other slowly, after a reflective pause. 'But I did hear there was a deep rift between the cattlemen of the Bar X ranch, the biggest in the territory and the townsfolk of Triple Peaks.'

'What inference are you drawin' from that?' Garth asked.

'Just that if Turrell wanted to bring in more recruits to swell his ranks and make sure that he could outfight any posse you could bring against him, he wouldn't be short of men. The Bar X men would side with him right away.'

'I had considered that, but I doubt if he'll have had time to lay any plans like that. Besides, the more men he has, the more shares with the spoils. He'll want to keep as much of the gold and dollar bills for himself as he can.'

'Could be,' admitted the other thoughtfully. He stretched himself in his chair, gave Garth an oblique glance. His forthright gaze was blacker now and unfathomable. He sat still for a further moment, then said: 'Reckon you'll be ready to hit the hay, Garth. I'll walk over to the hotel with you. Don't worry about your horse. I'll get one of the boys to take care of him for you.'

'Thanks.' Getting to his feet, Garth waited while the other gave his orders to the man lounging against the upright outside the office, then they walked slowly along the street. It was virtually deserted now, most of the men being in the saloons or the eating houses spaced at intervals along the sides of the main street. Culver City was an up-and-growing place. A few years before it had been merely a collection of wooden shacks, but now that the railroad had moved up to it and there was a railhead there for shipping cattle back east to the markets, it had grown overnight into a big, sprawling place of more than seven thousand head. Soon, unless he missed his guess, it might be one of the biggest and most important towns in this stretch of territory.

'I'll see you in the mornin' before you pull out,' Cantry said as they parted just outside the entrance of the hotel. 'You'll be all right here.'

'I'm sure I will,' Garth nodded. At that moment, all he wanted was to get his head down and sleep. The other waved his hand in salute, turned and walked out towards the outskirts of town, making his rounds of the place. Not that much was likely to happen there so long as the outlaws kept themselves further west, Garth mused as he went inside.

* * *

Garth ate his breakfast with the three other guests at the hotel, washed the

242

well-cooked food down with two cups of hot, black coffee, smoked a single cigarette and when he had finished, stepped outside into the cool air of the street. The sun had just risen and there was a pale, overall red glow in the thin, winey air.

Cantry appeared a hundred yards away, came towards him. He said: 'Saddle up when you're ready and I'll ride part of the way with you. There's somebody I have to see along the trail a piece.'

Garth went over to the livery stables for his horse and gear, threw the saddle on to the animal, tightened the cinch, checked the Winchester in its scabbard behind the saddlehorn, then swung up and rode out of the stables into the street. Cantry was outside the sheriff's office as he drew level with the building. He finished his conversation with a couple of deputies, then moved out on to the street, climbing into the saddle, and wheeled his mount along-side Garth's.

Together, they rode out of town, heading west, cutting out into the rough country that lay just beyond the town, where the trail ran up into a shelving area of ground, covered with flinty stones that made going difficult and treacherous for their horses. Cantry was silent for some time, his face set as he sat tall and easy in the saddle, staring straight ahead of him. Then, presently, he turned and threw Garth a quick, enigmatic glance.

'If you do succeed in smashing this outlaw band, what do you intend to do then, Garth?' he asked. 'Keep on ridin' over the hill? Out west?'

'Maybe,' he said quietly.

'We have a hard time getting good men to stay in these parts when we're lookin' for men to keep the law. Wouldn't you consider that?'

'You're forgettin' that I already have a job with the Rangers?'

'No, I'm not forgettin'. But I thought that you might think it over. It's no skin off my nose what happens in Triple

Peaks. But it does seem to me that they need a man there who could keep the law. Jessup is no use at all.'

'And you think the townsfolk there might elect me in his place?' asked Garth with a faint smile.

'I think there's a good chance of it, if you'd indicate that you were willin' to take the job. And I also think there's an excellent chance that Jessup would be only too glad to give it up, if he had the chance.'

Garth pressed his lips firmly together, his eyes speculative under the straight-drawn brows. It was something he had not considered. The job of a Ranger was the only thing that had seemed right for him after he had left the Army with the end of the war that had ravaged the states. He did not like or dislike Triple Peaks. It was as good and as bad as a score of other towns he had known along the trail. Certainly there came a time when a man felt the urge to put down roots, to stay in one place and not be continually riding a different trail. For a moment, his thoughts strayed to Rosarie Glynn, but he put the idea out of his mind almost at once, although he would have liked to dwell on the girl. There was a curious sense of warmth in his body when he thought of her, picturing her as she had been when he had last seen her, imagining again the warmth that had been in her voice when she had thanked him for saving her life and her father's.

The trail moved on out of the rugged terrain, looped between tall green walls of timber. It was first-growth pine, broad at the base, the trunks rising sheer and unadorned by branches for almost forty feet before the wide canopy of green opened out overhead. In places, the intertwining branches were so thick that they shut out the light of the sun, letting only a pale green glow filter through. It was cool riding under the trees and the sharply aromatic smell of the trees lay in their nostrils. Underfoot, fallen pine needles formed a thick carpet that muffled the sound of their horses as they rode through the timber, moving downgrade for a mile or more before Cantry suddenly reined his mount where a narrow trail led off from the main one, branching up among the trees.

'This is where I leave you, Garth,' he said, nodding towards the trail. 'If you need any help from me to round up these coyotes, just send a message and I'll come a-ridin' with a posse. I doubt if you'll get much help from Jessup. He'll ride if he's forced to because there's no other way out, but you'd be surprised how easy it is to be out hunting drunken Indians or non-existent outlaws when there's need for gettin' a posse together and go after Turrell and his gang.'

'I'll bear that in mind,' Garth said. He stretched out his hand, grasped the other's firm grip, then kicked spurs against his horse's flanks, rode swiftly along the wide trail. At a bend, he paused for a moment to look back. Cantry was still there, his mount motionless. The other lifted a hand in farewell and then rode up into the timber.

The trail was a solid streak of dust as the trees thinned on either side and he came out into more open country, to feel the full searing blast of the sunheat on his back and shoulders. There was still that sun-blasted desert to cross. When he came to it a little more than an hour later, with the sun lifting steadily and remorselessly to its zenith and the heat head piling up around him, he touched rowels to his horse, urging it on, now more in a hurry than ever.

Through all of the punishing labour of the afternoon, when each breath he took struck like fire in his lungs, searing his chest, he saw no one along the whole of the trail. The hills on the skyline shimmered and danced and the dust devils whirled across the still face of the desert like living things, entities possessed with life all their own. As he rode, he turned over in his mind all that he knew about this outlaw band, operating around Triple Peaks. He was sure in his own mind that Turrell was leading them. Only Ed Turrell would have the cunning, the experience, to carry out these attacks on banks and stages, and slip away into the hills like a ghost before he could be captured by the law. Only Turrell would set himself up against the law like this, deliberately choosing a place on the very frontier where things always favoured the crook and the gambler.

There was, he realized, only one way of trapping the other. To play on his greed and his belief that he was smarter than anybody else. He began to turn over in his mind various schemes for trapping Turrell and his men. There had to be a way.

The sun was just beginning to slide down from its zenith when he rode into the rolling swales, indicative of the more prominent upthrusts of ground ahead before he reached the hills. It hung in a faded brassy sky, sending the waves of heat rolling over the desert's dusty face, bringing all of the moisture in his body boiling to the surface, oozing from every pore. His horse began to slow now and he did not press it.

Topping a long, low gravelly ridge, he spotted the cluster of tumble-down weathered buildings less than a quarter of a mile from the trail. He did not recall seeing them before, then realised that he had ridden this way in total darkness. He was on the point of riding past when a second glance showed him smoke curling from a battered chimney and, acting on impulse, he wheeled his mount off the trail and cut over to the buildings.

He was fifty yards from them when he caught the sudden movement at the small window. A few moments later, the door opened and a white-haired man stepped out on to the broken-down porch, an ancient rifle in his hands. The barrel was pointed unwaveringly at Garth.

'Stay right where you are, mister,' said the other thinly. 'Come another step nearer and I'll let you have it.'

Garth reined up. He recognised the other's fear, his instant suspicion of strangers. Keeping his hands well spread from his body he leaned forward on the pommel horn and said quietly, evenly: 'Put up that rifle, old-timer. I just want to have a talk with you.'

'I got nothin' to say,' snapped the other. The barrel of the rifle continued to point at his chest and the spark of suspicion still flared in the other's eyes.

'Then you got any objection if I have a drink of water? It's been a long, thirsty ride across the desert.'

'All right, step down and help yourself.' The offer came grudgingly. The other gestured with the rifle towards the olla suspended from the corner of the porch. 'But don't make any funny moves towards your guns, or I'll pull this trigger.'

Sliding from the saddle, keeping his hands well in sight, Garth went over to the olla, upended it and drank until he could drink no more. The water was cool and slaked his thirst.

'If you've had enough, get back on your horse and ride on out of here,' said the other, continuing to watch him.

'Just what are you afraid of, old-timer?' Garth asked slowly. He fixed the other with his gaze. 'Outlaws?'

By the narrowing of the other's eyes, he knew that he had hit the mark. He went on quietly: 'I know there are outlaws operatin' in the hills yonder. It's part of my job to see that they're brought in for trial.'

'How do I know that, mister?' said the other. The suspicion was there, but he no longer sounded quite so belligerent. 'I ain't ever seen you before. You could be one of them for all I know.'

'Would I come ridin' in like this if I was?'

'No, maybe not,' agreed the other reluctantly. 'But that doesn't mean I'll help you. I know those critters. If they ever get to hear that I've given information to a lawman this hut would be burned down about my ears and there's little enough I have in the world now for me to want that to happen.'

'But you know somethin' about them, don't you?' Garth went on. He saw now that the other had lowered the rifle, that it was no longer pointed at his chest.

'Maybe,' said the other with a faint show of impatience. 'I see and hear a lot out here. I know more'n I dare tell. So far, they don't care about me. I'm just an old fool livin' out near the middle of the desert. But if they guessed how much I really do know, then they'd care and my life wouldn't be worth a plugged nickel.' There was a bright and beady wisdom in the other's eyes now in place of the suspicion.

'You know where they have their hide-out in the hills?'

'Nope.' The other shook his head at that and Garth knew instinctively that he was telling the truth. 'But I reckon they'll have got back there by now. The posse from Triple Peaks came by here ridin' hell for leather a while ago. They scouted this side of the hills, lookin' for a trail I guess, then turned and headed back.'

'You're sure they came from Triple Peaks?' Garth felt a little stab of apprehension run through him. What had happened while he had been away?

'I'd recognize Jessup anywhere,' he said thinly. 'Besides, the news is that they held up the bank in Triple Peaks a couple of days back, got away with all the gold they were carryin' in the vaults, shot one of the employees dead when he tried to stop 'em.'

Garth absorbed the news slowly, sucking in a sharp intake of air that betrayed his lack of knowledge. The other searched his face closely. 'You didn't know about that raid on the bank, then, stranger?'

'No. Like I told you. I've just ridden in from Culver City. I've been out of touch with things for the past four days.'

'Well, that's what happened, mister.' The other leaned the ancient Sharps rifle against the side of the porch. 'You a sheriff?'

Garth shook his head. 'Let's just say that I'm interested in bringing in these coyotes, dead or alive,' he answered.

The other studied him briefly and when next he spoke, his voice sounded bitter towards him. 'You're a lawman, no matter what you say. You want to avenge a murder with more murders. I've seen so much goddamned violence in my life that I came out here to get away from it all, if that's possible. But I've now found that to do that you have to get away from human beings. It's the only way.'

'Somebody has to bring in killers and outlaws,' Garth said defensively. This was an outlook, an attitude, and he was unsure how to deal with it. 'I know how you feel, but I've been a lawman for almost eight years now and I reckon

I've seen about every kind of killer there is. The worst kind are those who work behind masks, hiding their identity. They're cowards and if you don't stop them, they get around to thinkin' that they're brave and there's not many men more deadly on this earth than a deluded coward. Maybe someday the townsfolk of Triple Peaks will thank me for what I'm doin'.'

'Reckon you've got to catch the critters first,' said the other pointedly. He gave a slight chuckle, half-wise, half-foolish. 'You want a bite to eat? It's still mighty hot and you'll travel quicker when it gets cool.'

'Why, thanks, old-timer.' He followed the other into the shack. The meal was frugal, but filling and when it was over, Garth felt a sense of well-being, the gnawing hunger pains in his stomach having gone. As they went outside, the oldster said, calculatingly: 'If you do meet up with this *hombre* who leads these outlaws, don't jump at conclusions about him because he wears a patch over one eye. The man is better than he looks.'

'Thanks for the meal,' said Garth and stepped up into the saddle.

'You won't forget what I told you?'

'I won't forget,' said Garth, and rode off.

* * *

The afternoon was almost gone now and the heat head was beginning to diminish although very slowly. During most of the day nothing had relieved it. Even though he had rested up for that short period at the shack, the day had been a punishment to him, every breath he drew in a distinct labour in his lungs as they strove to extract sufficient oxygen from the superheated air for his needs. The edges of his saddle were now too hot for real comfort and the red rays of the setting sun were directly in his eyes, glinting off the metal pieces of his bridle.

A little before six o'clock, the country

lifted again. He ran into isolated clumps of trees warning him of his approach to the hills. Now they were black and menacing, brooding on the near horizon, with the setting sun throwing them into deep shadow on his side. Bulky and high, they loomed over the trail which was now only a thin, yellow streak through the dust, running over the last few miles of desert in a twisting, criss-cross fashion.

Although it would be dangerous to camp in the hills, he recognised that he had very little choice in the matter. His mount was in no condition to continue to ride west through the night. The day had been more of a punishment for it than it had been for him, and there was still a whole day's journey to travel once he got through the hills that stretched themselves across his path.

Turning off the trail once he was well into the foothills, with the sky darkening rapidly overhead, he made cold camp among the tangle of trees and thorn. Hobbling his mount, he settled out in his blankets, placing his gunbelt near the saddle which he used as a pillow. The ground was hard and moist under him and once it grew really dark and the coldness settled over the world, there was a rising, misty dampness in the air that chilled him to the marrow. Around him, the vague noises of nocturnal animals, rooting through the brush, kept him awake for a long while and when he finally did fall asleep, it was an uneasy doze from which he woke at intervals, listening for the sounds around him that would warn him of the approach of danger. Once, he jerked himself up on to his arms, every sense and nerve in his body straining as he caught the distant sound like a washboard being scrubbed with knuckles. A rider, moving along one of the many trails about him. As he listened, however, the sound faded into a dull murmur, then was gone altogether.

When he woke for the last time, he smoked a cigarette in the chill darkness and sat shivering in the cold, waiting for the steely palings of the dawn as they gradually streaked the eastern skies. Nearby, his mount grazed quietly. All about him the hills were still and hushed, a strange, foreboding quiet that began to eat at his nerves, stretching them taut.

As he smoked, he tried to think things out in the light of what the old man had told him the previous afternoon. It certainly altered things a little. If the outlaws had got away with all that gold, and killed a man in the process, the chances were that they had not headed back into these hills, but were even now riding hell for leather to the border. They must surely have realized that things were bound to get too hot even for them, that if they wanted to stay alive to spend any of the ill-gotten gains from their activities, the sooner they fled out of the country, the better. Sooner or later, their luck was going to run out. They could not continue to rob and murder with impunity much longer.

Eating the last of the strips of beef he had brought with him, washing it down with ice-cold water from a nearby stream, he saddled up, rode out with the dawn. Mountain shoulders sloped down towards him on both sides, cramping the dim trail he had chosen through the range. He had deliberately avoided the main stage trail through, just in case anyone was watching it. It seemed quite likely to him that the outlaws in these hills, out of a sense of mutual protection, would have a system of watching the main trails.

An hour after setting out, he rode down a narrow canyon whose steep-sided walls funnelled the wind along it endlessly and he smelled the faint scent of a cooking fire but when he rounded a bend in the trail and came in sight of the fire, he found it to be merely grey ashes that were not even warm. He wasted several precious moments quartering it though, just to be on the safe side, not wanting anyone on his back without him knowing of it. Then he rode on, up to the crests, over the top of a wide, high ridge and down the further side. Here and there, he spotted the decrepit wooden buildings of the old mine workings he had been told about, most of them with their roofs fallen in, no longer habitable; but once or twice, he spotted others which seemed to have been erected more recently, and he guessed that these places would afford shelter to the wanted ones who lived in these hills, away from the eyes of the law.

By the time he had reached the benchlands that opened out on to the wide prairie, black thunderheads were rising over the mountains in the distance and a black, filmy curtain of rain came sweeping forward out of the west. The sun still shone brightly at his back, but he knew it would be only a matter of time before the storm reached him and he huddled forward in the saddle, seeing no place here where he could possibly shelter from it, knew he was going to finish the rest of the journey back to Triple Peaks wet to the skin. He sighed, then put the thought out of his mind. A man liked to ride dry and in comfort, but nature was not like that and there were times when he had to grin and bear it.

The storm struck half an hour later. Preceding it, the wind rose, and there was a short period when it caught at the sand and dust and whipped it up into a thick, stinging cloud of irritating grains that beat furiously at him, whipping his clothing around his body, his chaps cracking like pistol shots. He rode with his head lowered, unable to see more than a few feet in front of him, relying on the horse to keep to the trail. Fortunately, the sand storm did not last for long. When the rain came, falling in large drops on his hat, it slaked the sand, brought down the dust. But even the rain, driven at him by the fierce force of the wind, made it impossible for him to see where he was headed, or even if he was still following the trail. It churned the ground into a quagmire of mud and ooze, the horse's hooves sinking deeply into it, splashing through the puddles that formed in the multitudinous hollows.

Lightning slashed and zigzagged across the berserk heavens and the thunderclaps were monstrous sounds that threatened to deafen him. This was elemental nature in the raw and at its most frightening. He rode without lifting his head, conscious only of the rage of the elements all about him.

8

Shoot-out

As he entered the main street of Triple Peaks, Jessup stepped down from the boardwalk and came over to him. He looked questioningly at him as Garth sat tall in the saddle.

'I never expected to see you ridin' in here again,' he said belligerently. 'When they told me at the hotel that you'd pulled out, I had you figured for the same kind of man as this fella Smith.'

'Now you see how wrong you were,' Garth said evenly, keeping all emotion out of his tone. He stepped down from the saddle, took off his wide-brimmed hat and shook it so that the water spilled from it in a cascade of glistening drops. He rubbed his face with the back of his hand. He felt tired and relaxed now that he had arrived in town. But he was totally unprepared for the sheriff's next question.

'And where did you leave your friends — out there in the hills, while you rode back to see if you could pick up some information? They must sure be wonderin' what we mean to do now?' There was no mistaking the harsh grimness in the sheriff's tone. He seemed to have taken on some of the hardness of the rest of the men in town.

'I don't know what you're talkin' about,' Garth said, matching the other's direct gaze.

'No? Then maybe I ought to refresh your memory. Those outlaw friends of yours rode into town four days ago and robbed the bank of all the gold in the vaults. But that wasn't all. They shot Abe Carlton. Plugged him in the chest. He never had a chance.'

'I heard about that,' Garth said, 'on my way here from Culver City. I'm sorry. But it only shows that we have to get some plan to destroy them before they can build up into something so big that we can't stop it short of bringin' in the troopers.'

'You're sorry!' There was scorn in the lawman's tone and he held his right hand just above the butt of his gun, fingers stiff-spread. 'And how come you heard about it if you've just ridden in from Culver City? That's a four-day ride, there and back.' His eyes narrowed, flaring in sudden suspicion.

'Easy there, Sheriff,' Garth said, and there was a tight note of warning in his tone. 'I stopped over with some old-timer in a shack this side of the desert. Seems he spotted you a couple of days ago when you rode the far side of the mountains. He noticed too that you never ventured into the hills after those killers.'

'You're talkin' pretty smart, Martinue,' snapped the other. His face was flushed with anger. 'But I've got a damned good mind to run you into jail on suspicion of being in cahoots with that gang. Maybe I should, just to be sure you don't ride out and join 'em with information.'

'And maybe you should try to think things out calmly and logically, Sheriff,' said Garth, forcing evenness into his tone. 'You could easily check if I'd been in Culver City by gettin' in touch with Sheriff Cantry there, so if I were in cahoots with these outlaws I wouldn't have told you that, would I?'

'I've already decided to get in touch with Cantry,' muttered the other. 'But I've had a message from him in response to a telegraph I sent to him a few days ago and he's never heard of you.'

'I can understand that,' Garth said. 'I told him myself not to say anythin' about me in his reply.'

'Now why would you want to do a thing like that?' There was a note of open disbelief in the other's voice now. He opened his mouth to say something more, but it was never said, for at that precise moment another voice cut in from the boardwalk.

'I think I can answer that, Jessup. If

you'd both step into your office.'

Jessup whirled, saw Wayne Thorpe standing a few feet away. For a moment, he hesitated, then shrugged his shoulders, nodded tersely, and stepped up on to the plankwalk, preceded the two men into his office and closed the door behind them. Tossing his hat on to the top of the desk, he motioned them towards the chairs in front of the long desk.

'All right, Thorpe. You seem to know a lot more about this than I do. Suppose you tell me what's on your mind.'

The lawyer crossed his legs and leaned back in his seat, eyeing the other shrewdly. Then he said quietly: 'No doubt you've been wondering, as a good many men in town have, who Martinue is, and why he's here.'

'And you know?'

'Certainly,' Thorpe nodded. 'I wired and asked him to come. By that time, I'd already realized that the situation here was rapidly getting out of hand

and that something had to be done to stop it. Recent events have only proved how right I was.'

'And Martinue here?' Jessup switched his gaze to Garth. There was still a hardness in it that the other noticed at once. Jessup was not an easy man to convince.

'He's a Texas Ranger — an old friend of mine. I've known him for several years, knew his father too. I reckoned that if I wired him, he'd come if he possibly could.'

Jessup's gaze altered subtly. 'I see.' He leaned back, clasped his hands together, fingers tightly interlocked. 'But I don't see how you're goin' to help us. We don't know where these men are hidin' out and if we tried to ride into those hills after them, we'd be cut down from ambush before we knew where they were. There are too many trails yonder for us to have a hope in hell of smokin' them out.'

'I'm inclined to agree with that,' Garth nodded. 'That means we must

employ some other means of catchin'
them. My idea is that we bring them
out into the open, back into Triple
Peaks. Then seal off every way of
escape.'

'Sounds good, but how do you figure
on doin' that?'

'They've already robbed the bank
here, so where do you think they may
strike next?'

Jessup shrugged. 'That could be
anybody's guess. They're cunnin'. They
will wait until they're sure they can
strike by surprise as they did the last
time.'

'Fine, Sheriff. But let us put ourselves into this man Turrell's place.'

'Turrell?' inquired Jessup, leaning
forward.

'That's the real name of this man
who called himself Smith when he was
here. He led a band of outlaws down on
the Texas border about a year ago until
it was smashed by the Rangers. He was
the only one to get away. The others
were either killed in the gunfight, or

taken prisoner and hanged. We've been lookin' over a dozen states for him, for a long time now. Until this moment, he's given us the slip.'

'And what do you think he'll do?'

Garth smiled tightly. 'I think he'll ask himself the question: where is the one place where the law will never expect him to strike? And there is only one answer to that, particularly if we can make things seem easy and tempting for him. Here, at the bank in Triple Peaks.'

Jessup stared at him, his jaw slackly open, a look of surprise on his bluff features. Even Thorpe seemed a little stunned by the other's statement.

'Here in Triple Peaks! But surely they — '

'They won't take us for fools. But I reckon it's obvious that nobody would expect them to hit the same place again, just after taking all of its gold.'

'And how are you goin' to convince them that it might be worth their while to come back here?'

'I'm sure they have somebody in town who feeds them news. You suspected it was me a little while ago, so the thought has obviously crossed your mind as well and I'm sure it's the truth. We must spread it around that a further consignment of gold has been brought and deposited in the bank here from Culver City for safe keepin'. That ought to convince them too that we're reasonably certain this is the one bank they won't attack again. But we must do this discreetly. Whatever happens, we mustn't make it too obvious or they won't fall for it. And there will have to be a shipment of some kind into the bank to back it up. Then we set the trap and wait for them to spring it.'

'I like the idea,' said Thorpe after a brief, reflective pause. 'I'm sure it's our only chance of getting them.'

'I'm not so convinced. If it doesn't work and we concentrate all of our men here, it could be givin' them the chance to hit someplace else and they would be able to rob and loot against no opposition at all.' Jessup frowned.

'I feel that's a calculated risk,' Garth said quietly. 'Unless you can think of a better idea. And you said yourself we'd have no chance at all goin' into those hills after them.'

Jessup was silent for a long moment, brows drawn close in furrowed thought. Then he allowed his shoulders to slump fractionally. 'Very well, I agree. But I still feel that we're makin' a big mistake.'

★   ★   ★

Two days later, a heavily guarded stage rolled into the main street of Triple Peaks. Five armed men rode with it and there was another riding shotgun on the box alongside the driver. Three more men rode inside the stage. It would have been obvious to anyone watching it along the trail from Culver City that it carried something mighty valuable and that no chances were being taken with outlaws attacking it on this particular trip.

Instead of proceeding to the way station, it pulled up outside the bank and five heavy boxes were carried inside under the watchful eyes of the armed guards. There was a small crowd gathered that early evening watching the proceedings with interest, the way in which Jessup fussed around the men carrying in the boxes like a broody old hen.

Fifty feet or so from the bank, the man lounging against one of the posts, his hat drooping over his eyes, seemed to be taking no interest at all in what was going on. He was, however, more interested than anyone there. Ten minutes after the stage had arrived in front of the bank, the driver climbed up on to the box, cracked the long whip over the backs of the horses and drove off to the depot while the guards waited until the bank had been securely locked and then moved off in a noisy bunch to the saloon to slake their thirst and wash the dust of the long journey out of their throats.

The man in the shadows waited patiently. He smoked a cigarette, ground the butt out in the dust at his feet and lit another as if he had all the time in the world. Then, casually, he dropped the second cigarette on to the street and turning, made his way to the stables, vanishing into the dark interior. Less than three minutes later, he rode out on a chestnut gelding, paused for a moment to look up and down the street and then rode off at a steady, unhurried trot out of town.

He rode out of town unnoticed, except for one man. Standing near the window of his room at the hotel, Garth watched the man ride out of Triple Peaks and there was a thin smile of satisfaction on his face as he turned away after watching the dark figure being swallowed up by the encroaching night.

The man rode hard once he left the town behind, taking the trail that led east. He rode through the night without stopping once, until he reached the dark foothills and then cut up along a twisting trail, splashing through half a dozen narrow streams before he finally came out on to the bare hillside that lifted steeply in front of him in long runs of loose gravel and shale. Here, he was forced to ride more slowly, knowing that one wrong move on the part of his mount and he could go plunging headlong down the slope, to end up at the bottom with a broken neck.

It was almost dawn when he finally rode through the timber, came out on to the upgrade that led to the mine workings, dimly seen in the pale light. He walked his mount now, knowing that the chances were he was being watched from the shacks directly ahead of him. He was less than thirty yards away, however, before a harsh voice rang out.

'Stay right there, mister.'

With an effort, he found his voice. 'It's me, Miguel,' he called back.

A pause, then a rock rattled down the slope and a dark shape materialised out of the gloom. Kreb slithered down the rock face, still gripping the Winchester in his huge paws.

'So it is, Miguel,' he said. 'We were expectin' you earlier. What kept you? Trouble in town?'

'No. But it is a long way here, and a long climb from the valley.'

Kreb laughed hoarsely. 'All the better for us to keep watch,' he said grimly. 'You'd better come along with me. Turrell is waitin' for your news.' He led the way up the slope, called out as they neared the low-roofed assay hut.

'Miguel is here, Turrell.'

'Bring him in.'

Thrusting open the door, Kreb ushered the Mexican into the hut. There was a lamp burning on the table and Turrell, the patch over his eye making him look more terrible than ever, was seated on the edge of one of the low bunks. He had evidently just wakened from sleep.

Motioning Miguel to a chair, he poured a drink from the whiskey bottle.

When the other had downed it, he said sharply: 'What did you find out in Triple Peaks?'

'The stage came in last evening. I don't know what it was they were carrying, Señor Turrell. But they had nine men guarding it and they took five boxes into the bank, locked them away there. Jessup was keeping an eye on the proceedings.'

'I can imagine that,' muttered Turrell grimly. He nodded his head, however, and there was a look of intense satisfaction on his face. 'That was gold they were shippin' into Triple Peaks from the bank at Culver City.'

'Gold.' There was astonishment in Miguel's voice as he stared at the other and then poured himself a second drink. 'But that is impossible, señor. They would not be such fools. The gold was taken out of the bank in Triple Peaks by you only a few days ago. Surely they, would not be so stupid as to — '

Turrell shook his head. 'They're not

stupid, Miguel. They're bein' as clever as they know how. They reckon that we'll not attack that bank a second time, so soon after the first. They think that we do not know of the stage, but they were not too careful when they passed through the mountains. I have ways of knowin' everythin' that goes through the trails here. We saw the stage pass through early yesterday afternoon. Now you've told me everythin' I want to know.'

'Then we are goin' after that gold,' said Kreb thinly. It was more of a statement of intent than a question.

Turrell gave a quick nod. 'We'll take it tonight. Before they expect anythin',' he said. 'Wake the others.'

'And Tragge. Does he ride with us. That shoulder of his — '

'That shoulder is healed sufficiently now for him to be able to stay in the saddle. I need all of you. This will be the last raid we make. After this, we head south for the border. Once we're in Mexico, nobody can touch us. We'll live like kings.' There was a note of muted excitement in his tone.

* * *

All afternoon, Garth had been holed up with Jessup in the other's office. Slowly, the heat-filled hours had passed and still there had come no word from the men watching the trails into town that Turrel and his men were on their way. Gradually, he was beginning to feel the first stirring of doubt in his mind, knew that Jessup had already decided that his plan had failed, that Turrell had been too smart again to fall for the trap they had so carefully laid for him.

'You're sure that man who rode out of town was headed east?' Jessup asked, the same question he had put to the other for the dozenth time that afternoon.

Garth gave a quick nod. 'I'm sure of it. He was standin' there at the corner pretendin' not to be interested, and yet he was noticing everythin' that went on.

My bet is that he rode out to tell Turrell.'

'Then if that's so, why hasn't he shown up? Unless he's outsmarted us, knows it's a trap. A trick to lure him here.'

Garth shook his head very slowly. 'I don't think so. Besides, we've got to remember that this man would not reach their hide-out in the hills until about dawn even if he rode his hardest all the way. They may not have set out right away, although I have a feelin' that this time, Turrell will wait until it's dark before he attacks.'

'And that's why you had men workin' in the bank after dark? To give the idea they were checkin' the gold after normal opening hours.'

'Exactly.' Garth rose to his feet, went over to the window and glanced up and down the street. It looked deserted. There was an expectant hush lying over the whole town, as if it were waiting with bated breath for something to happen. So long as Turrell didn't notice it when he came riding in.

Jessup took out his watch and glanced down at it, then shoved it back into his pocket with a loud sigh. He hitched his gunbelt higher about his waist, walked over to the door. 'I'm goin' along to the saloon for a drink,' he said harshly. 'If anythin' should come up you can send one of the men over for me.'

Opening the door, he stepped out on to the boardwalk, then paused. There was the unmistakable sound of a rider spurring his mount at full speed into town. Garth was at the door beside the sheriff before the rider had reached them. The other slid from the saddle on the run letting the reins droop over his horse's neck.

'Bunch of men headin' for town, Sheriff,' he called excitedly. 'I spotted them from the top of the ridge.'

'How far?' asked Garth before the sheriff could speak.

'About three miles, I reckon.'

'Good. And you're sure they didn't see you?'

'Not a chance, Mister Martinue. The sun was in their eyes and I kept down all the time.'

'Could you judge how many there were?' broke in Jessup.

'Not accurately, Sheriff,' replied the other. 'Maybe half a dozen. Not many more, I'd say.'

'Sounds like them,' agreed Jessup. He pressed his lips tightly together. 'I'd better go and warn the rest of the boys.'

'Do they all know what to do as soon as I give the signal?' Garth asked.

'They've all been told,' Jessup nodded. 'We've got every damned road and alley leading off from the area of the bank sealed off with men. A fly couldn't get out without bein' seen.'

'I hope you're right. We want to get every goddamned one of them this time. Especially Turrell. He's the brains behind the outfit. With him dead or in jail, the others won't amount to anythin'.'

Jessup strode off along the street to warn the rest of his men. Garth paused for a moment outside the sheriff's office, then turned to go in the direction of the bank. He had taken only a dozen steps when a voice said softly: 'Be careful, Garth. These men are dangerous. They'll shoot it out when you trap them at the bank and — '

'I'll be careful,' he said, his voice equally soft.

'Does it have to be this way?' Rosarie asked, almost breathlessly.

'I'm afraid it does. It's the only way we can rid the territory of them. If we don't act now, then they'll grow and in a few short weeks nothin' we can do will stop them.'

'Somehow I knew when you came into town that it would end this way.' Her tone sounded strangely helpless, as though she recognised that there were forces acting here against which she could not possibly fight. She looked down at her clasped hands, then lifted her face shyly to his. 'Can I ask a favour of you, Garth?'

'Of course.' He nodded, wondering what was on her mind.

'When all this is over, stay here in Triple Peaks and take over the post of sheriff from Jessup.'

He smiled a little at that. 'Now what makes you think that Jessup would want to give up this job even if I was willing to take it?' he asked.

'I know he would. He isn't cut out to be a lawman, even though he often tries hard. We need a man who isn't afraid to stand up to trouble when it comes, who doesn't sit around and try to figure out which is the best way of avoiding it, but goes out and meets it head-on. A man like you, Garth.'

His smile widened just a little. 'Maybe you don't know it, Rosarie, but I already have a job as a Texas Ranger. I'm a little far from my stamping grounds I'll admit, but — '

'But nothing. If we need you here, on the frontier, then I'm sure you could come.'

He turned towards her, surprised by

the vehemence in her voice. In that moment, she loosened her hands and lifted them around his neck, pressing him close to her. He felt the warm, soft pressure of her lips on his. Then she had drawn away, pushing herself gently from his enfolding arms.

'Please be careful, Garth . . . '

Placing his hand under her chin, he tilted it slightly upward, looked down into her eyes. 'I'll be careful, Rosarie,' he said quietly; 'and you be waiting.'

He moved away then, not looking back once, knowing without doing that, that she had remained standing there, looking after him. He found Jessup near the bank. There was no sign of the rest of the men, but Garth knew that they were there, out of sight, but ready once the outlaws put in an appearance.

'Let's get ourselves out of sight,' Garth said, taking the other's arm. 'Now that it's dark, my guess is that they won't waste time ridin' in.' He glanced across the street to where yellow lights glowed behind the windows of the bank. Except for this, the entire part of town here might have been utterly deserted. That, he thought to himself, was the impression they wanted to give to Turrell and his men; the impression they had to give if they were to be successful in springing this trap.

The dark body of clustered horsemen slowed down as they reached the edge of town, walked their horses quietly forward once they entered Triple Peaks. Except for the gravelly sound of their horses' hooves in the dust as they passed along, there was not a single sound in the night. From his vantage point, Garth counted them as they rode close enough for him to see them clearly. Only five of them. He felt a tight sense of exultation. It was not usual for him to count his cattle before they were branded, but it seemed that this time, there ought to be no mistake.

The riders halted in front of the bank. Garth could see that they seemed to be a trifle uneasy. Maybe, it was the quiet that did this. The expectant quality hanging over the town was enough to give any man pause. Then, as if in answer to a unspoken prayer, a drunk staggered out of the saloon a hundred yards along the street, a bottle clutched in his right hand, holding it high in the air over his head. Staggering, he wove unsteadily from one side of the street to the other, moving away from the silent men on horseback.

It was almost as if the tension that had gripped the five men had slipped from them visibly like a cloak. They swung down from the saddle and advanced slowly on the bank. Their guns were drawn and while one of them, huge and black-bearded, stood outside, leaning against an upright, the other four men thrust open the doors and went inside.

Garth smiled grimly to himself. The trap was ready to snap shut. Those men inside the bank would find nobody there although the lights were burning, would find nothing but sand in the boxes inside the vaults.

A minute later, the four men appeared at the door of the bank. Turrell yelled something harshly at the top of his voice, made to move out on to the boardwalk, then stepped back as Garth levelled his gun on him and squeezed the trigger. He felt the Colt jump in his hand, jerking against his wrist. The slug whined through the doorway where Turrell had stood a split second earlier.

At the signal, the rest of the men opened fire, pouring a withering hail of lead in through the door and windows of the bank. The big man flopped to his knees, clutched at his chest, then drew deep down within himself on some strange reserve of strength, pushed himself up on to his knees, and lifted the gun in his right hand. He fired two shots across the street before he fell forward on to his face, rolling off the boardwalk into the dusty street, arms stretched out in front of him.

The other four men had gone down out of sight behind the door and windows. During a brief lull in the firing, Garth yelled: 'You don't have a chance, Turrell. Every trail out of town is sealed. Throw out your guns and come out with your hands lifted. You'll all get a fair trial.'

'Why don't you come in and take us?' called a voice from the bank. There was the brief stabbing of orange flame, tulipping out of the darkness. Slugs smashed into the wood near Garth's head and he pulled himself down behind the barrel in front of him, pausing to reload. One of the men a few feet from him suddenly coughed harshly and toppled forward, his gun falling from his fingers.

For several minutes the fusillade of shots crashed into the bank. Garth waited until he saw a sudden movement near the open doorway as one of the men moved his body slightly to get a better sight across the street. He waited for just a second longer, then squeezed off a couple of shots. A loud cry went up in the midst of the racket and the figure of a man, weaving drunkenly, staggered into view from the doorway of the bank, walked a couple of paces, then sank down on to the edge of the boardwalk as though tired. He remained there for a moment before toppling sideways.

For a long moment a deadly silence pulsed over the street. Then Garth called: 'You goin' to give in now, Turrell?'

There was no answer from the three men still holed up inside the bank. When there was still no answer as he repeated the question, he got slowly to his feet, waved the men on the side of the square forward. They closed in silently on the bank.

With every step he took, Garth expected to hear the silence of the night blown apart by a sudden gunshot, but none came. The silence lengthened and grew more ominous as it went on. Reaching the door, he stepped over the body of the man who lay on the boardwalk, kicked the door open and stepped inside, his gun swivelling to cover anybody who might be there. Glass lay everywhere, littering the floor.

Behind him, Jessup moved in, looked about him, jerked up his gun as he spotted the two men lying behind the windows, then lowered it again as Garth went forward and turned the men over with the toe of his boot, staring down into the dead faces, the wide eyes that looked up at him, unseeing in the yellow lamplight.

'Turrell there?' asked Jessup harshly.

'No, he isn't,' muttered Garth, his voice sharp. 'But he must be somewhere around. Get your men in here to search every room in the building. He can't have got away. He must be hidin' somewhere. If he doesn't give himself up, warn your men to shoot to kill.'

Jessup turned, motioned some of the men inside. He pointed to the door at the far end of the room, opened his mouth to issue the necessary orders, then stopped abruptly as a window suddenly crashed and a man's high-pitched voice from somewhere outside yelled: 'There he is! He's gettin' away!'

Swiftly, Garth ran for the door, aware that Jessup was pounding along at his heels. One of the men in the street pointed along the dark alley that ran alongside the bank building. He shouted: 'He ran that way, Sheriff. I'm sure it was Turrell.'

'He won't get far,' Jessup said thickly. 'There are men watching down there.'

'Maybe so, but they'll be lookin' for a man on horseback. He could move past them in the darkness.'

Turning, Garth ran for one of the horses, swung up into the saddle. As he rode towards the mouth of the alley, Jessup yelled at the top of his voice. 'Hold your fire down there, men. Martinue is coming through.'

Garth put the horse into the alley, kicking savagely at it with his heels. The thought that, after all their planning,

Turrell might still get away, almost broke him in half. At the end of the alley, he spotted the man standing there with a Winchester across his arms. Reining up, he called to the other:

'Did you see anybody come through here in the last few minutes?'

'Somebody came runnin'. He said he was from Jessup. Warned me to watch out for anybody on horseback. I was drawing a bead on you when the sheriff shouted.'

Garth smiled grimly. Turrell had certainly not missed a trick. He had got away into the darkness on the edge of town and he had tried to make it certain that anyone following him on horseback would be shot by one of their own men. Urging the horse onward, he rode among the low-roofed buildings, casting about him for any sign of movement, riding more slowly now, knowing that if Turrell had not decided to run for the open country where he might hide in the darkness, he would have hidden himself in one of these empty buildings. This part of town was a veritable warren of alleys and a nest of abandoned buildings, in any one of which the other could have gone to earth, knowing that there would be pursuit very soon.

But although he strained his eyes and ears, he could locate no one there. Five minutes later, he came to the edge of town, reined up his mount and peered out into the clinging darkness that lay over the countryside. If Turrell had gone running out there, it would be impossible to find him in the darkness unless he mobilised most of the townsfolk with torches. That way they might be able to smoke him out, run him to earth.

He was on the point of turning back to enlist the help of the townsfolk when his keen hearing picked up the faint scrape in the near distance. He leaned forward in the saddle, straining his ears. Then the sound was repeated and this time, he knew exactly what it was, the scrape of a man's boots on rock. Turrell was out there and not more than fifty or a hundred yards away.

Slowly, he walked the horse forward. In the palely shimmering starshine, now that his eyes were becoming accustomed to the darkness, he was able to pick out shapes. A clump of mesquite here and a stunted thorn there, with a long, low ridge that ran from right to left across his path. A moment later, he caught the furtive movement at the very edge of his vision. Turning his head, he saw the figure that eased its way cautiously over the uneven ground.

'All right, Turrell,' he said sharply, his voice sounding oddly loud in the stillness. 'Hold it right there.'

'You'll never take me.' The other turned, twisted and tried to run.

Dropping from the saddle, Garth moved after him. For a moment, he lost him in the shadows, then picked him out again as he ran over the ridge. Moving around to cut the other off, he saw Turrell dart across an open space devoid of vegetation, then suddenly drop his gun, throw up his arms and fall to his knees.

Garth closed in, keeping his gaze fixed on the other. 'Stand quite still, Turrell,' he snapped. 'This is as far as you go.'

The other paused, turned slowly. 'Do I get an even break?' he said tightly. 'You're not goin' to take me back alive. Either you give me a chance to go for my gun, or you'll have to shoot me in the back. I'm sure that will give you a good reputation.'

Garth hesitated. Then he thrust the Colt back into its holster, stood with his legs braced slightly apart, his right shoulder a little lower than the left.

'Get your gun then,' he said thinly. 'And when you do, use it.'

He saw Turrell move forward slowly to where the gun lay among the rocks. Almost too late, he saw that the other did not intend to go for it, that he had another gun in a shoulder holster. He saw Turrell's right hand cut down for it, diving diagonally across his body. The move took him by surprise. Only instinct saved him then. As his hand clawed for the gun in his holster, he threw his body sideways, hitting the ground hard, with a blow that almost stunned him, knocking all of the wind from his lungs. The gun in his hand, lifting towards the other, exploded in the same instant as the small Derringer in Turrell's hand. Garth felt the wind of the slug as it whistled past his head and ricocheted with a shrill screech off the rocks. He saw Turrell draw himself up on to his tiptoes as if straining to reach up for something high over his head. Then the Derringer fell from his fingers as if he lacked the strength to retain his grip on it. Arching his body, he fell forward on to his face among the rocks and lay still.

Going forward, Garth turned him over, then whistled up the horse and lifted the dead body of the outlaw across the saddle. Holding the reins, he walked the horse and its burden back into Triple Peaks. In the main street, there was scarcely a sound from the assembled townsmen until he appeared in the gloom, fully recognizable.

Then Jessup came forward.

'You'd better take him along to the mortuary,' Garth told him. 'He's all yours.'

After the other had taken the reins from him, he made his way slowly along the quiet street. Behind him, somebody had struck a note on a piano in one of the saloons. It would not take Triple Peaks long to realise that the era of Patch-Eye Turrell was ended. Maybe someday conditions here on the frontier might be different; yet until then men would have to continue to fight for what they believed to be right — and women would have to sit and wait and wonder.

He turned off the street, walked through the small wooden gate up to the house that stood a little way off the road. Rosarie had evidently heard the click of the gate, for she opened the door before he got there and stepped out on to the porch to meet him. She smiled mistily at him as he stepped forward, then held out her hands to him.

'I heard the shooting,' she said quietly. 'It's all over now?'

He nodded slowly. 'It's all over,' he said equally softly.

THE END

We do hope that you have enjoyed reading this large print book.

Did you know that all of our titles are available for purchase?

We publish a wide range of high quality large print books including:
Romances, Mysteries, Classics
General Fiction
Non Fiction and Westerns

Special interest titles available in large print are:
The Little Oxford Dictionary
Music Book, Song Book
Hymn Book, Service Book

Also available from us courtesy of Oxford University Press:
Young Readers' Dictionary
(large print edition)
Young Readers' Thesaurus
(large print edition)

For further information or a free brochure, please contact us at:
Ulverscroft Large Print Books Ltd.,
The Green, Bradgate Road, Anstey,
Leicester, LE7 7FU, England.
Tel: (00 44) **0116 236 4325**
Fax: (00 44) **0116 234 0205**

RODEO RENEGADE

Ty Kirwan

When English couple Rufus and Nancy Medford inherit a ranch in New Mexico, they find the majority of their neighbours are hostile to strangers. Befriended by only one rancher, and plagued by rustlers, the thought of returning to England is tempting, but needing to prove himself, Rufus is coached as a fighter by a circus sharp shooter, the mysterious Ghost of the Cimarron. But will this be enough to overcome the frightening odds against him?

GAMBLER'S BULLETS

Robert Lane

The conquering of the American west threw up men with all the virtues and vices. The men of vision, ready to work hard to build a better life, were in the majority. But there were also work-shy gamblers, robbers and killers. Amongst these ne'er-do-wells were Melvyn Revett, Trevor Younis and Wilf Murray. But two determined men — Curtis Tyson and Neville Gough — took to the trail, and not until their last bullets were spent would they give up the fight against the lawless trio.

MIDNIGHT LYNCHING

Terry Murphy

When Ruby Malone's husband is lynched by a sheriff's posse, Wells Fargo investigator Asa Harker goes after the beautiful widow expecting her to lead him to the vast sum of money stolen from his company. But Ruby has gone on the outlaw trail with the handsome, young Ben Whitman. Worse still, Harker finds he must deal with a crooked sheriff. Without help, it looks as if he will not only fail to recover the stolen money but also lose his life into the bargain.